THE LIVING DEAD BOY

AND THE ZOMBIE HUNTERS

a novel by Rhiannon Frater

The Living Dead Boy and the Zombie Hunters
By Rhiannon Frater

ISBN10 - 1453608842
ISBN13 - 9781453608845

Edited by Felicia A. Tiller
Cover art and design by Phillip R. Rogers
Interior formatting by Kody Boye

AUTHOR'S NOTE:
To Parents and Adult Readers

A long time ago, as I sat at my desk typing away on a new story, I had Rob Zombie's "Living Dead Girl" blasting away on my speakers. My nephew, who was around four at the time, came running into the room, began dancing, and singing "living dead boy" at the top of this lungs.

And that is how this story got its name.

My nephew is now in his early teens, a zombie fanatic, and one of the coolest kids I have ever known. He's got a great sense of humor and charm to boot. I told him about my idea of a little boy and his friends fighting off zombies and he said, "Oh, a story about me."

Well, this story isn't about my nephew, Brandon, but it is inspired by him.

Whenever he visits, I watch him play zombie games and he watches zombie movies with me. He often tells me what he would do if the zombies show up. When his younger cousin, J.T. visits at the same time, there is plenty of smack talking about how they would handle zombies. Even my lovely niece, Jacqueline, gets in on it.

My favorite memory of their last visit was when they pretended they were in the infected like in *28 Days Later* and leaped on my brother. Scary!

This story had been germinating in my mind for a very long time. My nephews and niece all encouraged me to write a story about kids and zombies. The three eldest children of two of my brothers are zombie obsessed. Even my youngest niece, who is only four at this time, is fascinated by zombies and the undead. *The Corpse Bride* is her favorite movie and toy.

Dr. Pus of the Library of the Living Dead podcast and press loved the story when I told it to him over the phone.

"Kids need a zombie story, too!" Dr. Pus declared.

So that is how Josh and his Zombie Hunters came into existence.

This is a story about kids and zombies, so it is not

all fun and games. It is a horror story and people will die. It's ***not*** *Home Alone meets the Zombies* with a lot of laughs. It's about every day kids suddenly facing the zombies they thought were so cool and realizing things are not quite as they imagined. They learn how to survive and be heroes in a way they never dreamed of.

My goal while writing was that a twelve year old and adult could read and love the story. I believe I have succeeded.

Rhiannon Frater, aunt to the living dead boy

June 12, 2010

Dedicated with much love to Brandon, the original living dead boy

and

J.T. Jacqueline, and Gabriella.
You are the original Zombie Hunters.

Heartfelt appreciation to Dr. Pus.
This story is also dedicated to the memory of your amazing father. He inspired me when writing about Josh's dad.

Special thanks to my fans. Your support has been a source of inspiration.

And, as always, loving thanks to my mother and husband for their constant encouragement.

CHAPTER 1

Josh could feel his muscles tensing as the zombie shuffled across his backyard in relentless pursuit. Setting his feet apart, the twelve-year-old lifted his weapon higher over his head. Despite the cool spring air, sweat trickled down the bridge of his nose.

The zombie let out a low moan, its gray-mottled hand lashing out at him.

"C'mon, you undead turd head!"

The zombie moaned again, twisting its head back

and forth, trying to focus on him. Its gruesome face was torn, revealing its yellow, broken teeth. Josh could hear the voices of his friends as they screamed instructions from the nearby clothesline, but he ignored them to focus on the creature bearing down on him. Taking deep breaths, he narrowed his gaze under his cap. His fingers, slick with sweat, tightened around the bat.

The zombie lurched forward, reaching out with a guttural growl. Its gnarled hands almost snagged him before he realized that he had underestimated its speed. With a shout, Josh swung the bat as hard as he could, slamming it into the side of the zombie's head.

"Owwwwwwwww!" the zombie screamed, falling to his knees, gripping his head. "That hurt, Josh!"

"Oh, man, I'm sorry!" Josh instantly tossed the foam bat away, feeling the rush of adrenaline still pumping through his body.

Peals of laughter erupted from nearby, and Josh threw his friends a nasty look. Leaning down, he pulled the zombie mask off his best friend.

Arturo's sweating face came into view. "That hurt, turd head!"

"Dude, I said I'm sorry. I don't know my own strength! I didn't think I would hit you that hard. You freaked me out, dude."

"Man, this hurts!" Arturo touched his swelling cheek. "My Mom is going to kill me!"

"Great swing, chump," Troy shouted at Josh, laughing hysterically.

"Gawd, Josh, why don't you just kill him?" Roger, Troy's brother, added.

The boys stood side by side laughing. Troy was adopted from Haiti and was named after Troy Aikman. Roger was named after Roger Staubach and was adopted from Cambodia. The brothers' parents were diehard Dallas Cowboy fans and the boys wore team jerseys with the names of their parents' heroes across their shoulders.

Shoving his straight black hair back from his brow, Roger crossed his eyes. "That's what you look like, Arturo. I think he scrambled your brains."

"They're rotten anyway." Troy grinned, and high-fived his brother.

Josh scowled at both of them as he helped Arturo up. The brothers thought they were hilarious; he thought they were annoying. But then again, they were both still in single digits at the age of nine. They had yet to reach his double-digit maturity level.

“Josh, seriously, my Mom is gonna kill me!” Arturo touched his cheek again, wincing.

“Look, just tell her that you ran into something.” He could already tell how this was going to go down. His Mom would get a phone call and all hell would break loose. She was already agitated enough over all the money problems his family was having.

“Josh, I can’t lie to my Mom. She can always tell when I’m lying, and then I really get it.”

“Well, the last time you got hurt playing zombies and survivors, she didn’t let you play with us for a week,” Josh reminded him. He pulled the plastic zombie-hand gloves off Arturo’s hands, feeling more than a little annoyed with the whole situation. “C’mon, let’s get back to training. We gotta be ready when the zombies come."

"Dude, zombies aren't real. Chill out. This is just for fun." Troy shook his head dramatically, his hair bobbing around his head like a cloud. He had a pretty good size Afro going. His adoptive parents were white and determined that their children embrace their heritage. Roger sported a bowl haircut that got him beat up by the older kids at school on a regular basis. The boys were probably lucky their parents were such diehard fans of the Cowboys, or they might have gotten stuck wearing native garb. Josh knew the boys had to eat food from their native countries once a week when they'd rather eat McDonald's.

"Zombies might be real," Josh corrected. "There is some weird stuff going down. I'm sure they're coming."

"How can you be so sure, turd breath?" Arturo kept poking at the puffy flesh on his cheek, wincing while doing it.

"I'm paying attention, that's how I know!" Josh sighed, then shook his head. "Yeah, I used to just like zombies because they were scary and cool, but now I think they are really coming. I want us to be ready."

"Your dad could just shoot them in the head," Roger pointed out. "He's got lots of guns and he's a soldier."

"He was a soldier."

"He still has guns," Arturo insisted.

Josh pushed his bangs out of his face and looked around his backyard. The other zombie in his training exercise was missing. "Yeah, but he...he...he doesn't like using them."

The big oak tree creaked and moaned above him as the wind sent the boughs into motion. The Zombie Fighters Headquarters remained securely tucked into the branches of the tree. The old one had fallen during a cold front, but his dad had helped them build a better, sturdier tree house for their base of operations.

"He still has guns. He can still kill 'em," Troy said firmly. "My parents don't like guns. They don't even own them. But your dad does, so he'll use them."

"Yeah, he'll head shot them!" Arturo exclaimed.

Roger made a big show of being shot in the head, his hand flying out dramatically from his temple to show the spray of brains, then fell to the ground.

"Drake, come out. We're not playing anymore," Josh called out. He didn't want to talk about guns or his dad. There was a lot he had overhead when his parents were up late arguing. Ever since his Dad had come home after the war in Iraq ended, he had been different. Something bad had happened, Josh was sure of it. "Drake! Come out!" The last thing he needed was his little turd of a brother disappearing on his watch.

Troy pretended to get shot by what looked like machine gun fire before flopping over his brother's "dead" body. Not to be left out, Arturo took several imaginary rounds to the chest before falling to the ground.

Josh ignored the make believe battle around him and began to scan the bushes along the fence line for his little brother. "C'mon, Drake! Come out.

We're not training anymore."

A knot formed in his gut as he again swept his gaze over the family swing and slide playscape his Dad had made out of scrap wood. Maybe Drake was hiding up on the platform. He wasn't supposed to climb up that high without Josh watching him. If he fell down, Josh would be in a world of trouble.

Nearby, his friends were getting up and pretending to get shot again. The deaths were growing more dramatic. He would have found them funny if not for the missing Drake.

"Drake!" His mom would kill him if anything bad happened to his little brother.

Josh began to jog toward the playset, terrified that Drake had managed to get up there wearing the zombie mask and had fallen down the slide.

"Drake!"

A tiny form darted out of the nearby bushes, grabbed his hand, and bit down.

"UGH!"

Josh stumbled back, shocked as pain gripped him. Jerking his hand back, he sent his attacker sprawling. The small zombie hit the ground and immediately burst into tears.

"Dammit, Drake! You weren't supposed to really bite me!"

"Yeah, he was," Troy pointed out from where he lay on the ground, emulating a dead zombie. "You told him to be a zombie. Zombies bite."

Josh rubbed the indentations in his hand irritably as he knelt down next to Drake. The three-year old's crying was muffled by the plastic zombie mask. It was made for an adult and its gaping maw was big enough to expose the bottom half of Drake's face. Josh could see his brother's head was turned to the side as he sobbed inside the hideous mask. It was one of Josh's favorites with its dangling eyeball and missing jaw.

"You hurt me," Drake sobbed. "I'm... gonna... tell."

"I'm sorry, Drake," Josh said, trying not to sound annoyed. He pulled the mask off his brother's head and the younger boy's golden curls glinted in the fading Texas sunlight. "I didn't mean to hurt you."

"...gonna...tell..."

"Don't be a wussy, Drake," Troy called out.

"Yeah, Drake. Be a man," Arturo added.

Roger remained dead on the ground.

"not...a man...want...to...be...the...baby..." Drake sniffled.

"C'mon. Get up before Mom comes out," Josh ordered.

"No."

"Drake, c'mon!"

"No, I'm the baby. You hurt me."

The screen door to the back porch swung open. "Josh? What's wrong with your brother?"

With a sigh, Josh looked up to see his mother standing on the cement steps that led up to the house. Her hand was on one hip and her blond hair, the same color as Drake's, was hanging around her face in soft curls.

"Get up, wimp," Josh hissed, trying to pull his brother up.

Drake let out a howl that sounded worse than any movie zombie.

“Great,” Josh sighed, resigned to the verbal tongue lashing that was coming.

“Josh! What happened? What did you do to your brother?”

His mother launched herself off the steps and ran into the yard. Josh clutched the zombie mask tightly in his hand as she neared him. Drake was still sobbing, but Josh could tell it was fake. This was just his luck. His zombie training had gone wrong, and now his brother was going to get him in trouble.

Sweeping Drake up into her arms, his mom gave Josh a stern expression. “Okay, enough of all this. Get your stuff together and come inside. Dinner is soon anyway. Your Dad will be home any minute now.”

“Fine,” Josh grumbled. He felt humiliated in front of his friends. It was rough being the leader of his motley crew of Zombie Hunters and it didn’t help to be chastised by his mother.

“Okay, boys. You better head home. I’m sure it is almost your dinner time, too.” Cradling Drake against her, his mom walked back toward the house. "Hurry up, Josh. And we'll talk about how you need to take care of your brother and not pick on him when you get inside."

Exhaling slowly, trying to keep his temper, Josh watched his mother disappear back into the old house. Drake smiled and waved over her shoulder at him.

"Little pest," Josh muttered.

"Your Mom is so hot," Arturo said in awe.

"No, she's not."

"Uh huh," Troy corrected.

"Very hot," Roger agreed.

"She's just a stupid mom," Josh groused. "I better get inside." He grabbed up his zombie masks and the zombie gloves as the other boys began to pick up their stuff.

"See ya tomorrow at school, Josh," Troy called out as the boys headed to the back gate.

Josh trudged along behind his friends trying hard not to let the resentment he felt growing in his chest overwhelm him. He hated that his little brother could get him in trouble so easily, and he hated it that his friends didn't take his training sessions seriously. Shoving his damp bangs off his forehead, he sighed dramatically.

"Look, dude, at least there aren't real zombies," Arturo said as he paused at the gate. The shorter boy grinned at him, flashing all his white teeth.

"Yeah, playing zombies is cool, but it would not be cool if they were real," Troy agreed.

"That would super-suck in a big way." Roger pulled the gate open. "They'd be all...smelly...and nasty."

"Superman could totally kick their butt," Arturo decided.

"Or Spider-man," Troy said, quickly standing up for his favorite superhero.

"Didn't all the superheroes go zombie in the Marvel comics?" Roger asked.

"Superheroes aren't real, so they wouldn't help us with zombies," Josh answered. "And yeah, Marvel has the superheroes be zombies. And that's lame. Superman is the man of steel. They couldn't bite him." Josh felt confident in this proclamation. He had yet to actually see the comics, but he was hoping to one day read them.

"Well, zombies aren't real either, so we're safe," Arturo declared.

"That's the thing, Arturo. I think they are real. I watch the Zombie Tracker forum every day and there are some really weird news stories going on out there. Really weird! They're not fake either. I looked them up on CNN and MSNBC. They were real news stories. I think something really super-bad is happening and the government is hiding it. That's why I keep trying to get you guys to train. This isn't a game anymore."

"Chill out, man." Troy shook his head. "C'mon. Even our parents would be all paranoid and loading up on ammo and stuff if they thought we were in danger."

"Yeah, my Mom freaks if I sneeze," Arturo agreed. "She'd go buy a bazooka or something."

"And your Dad would probably be recalled to Fort Hood," Roger added, vigorously rubbing his nose. He was always sneezing and having trouble with his allergies. "They'd be boarding up the windows like in *Night of the Living Dead.*"

"Yeah, well, sometimes parents are stupid," Josh answered grimly. His mom never wanted to hear anything about zombies or his theories on a government conspiracy to hide their evil experiments that had created the zombies. "And they can be total douches."

That brought on some snickers of agreement then his friends were out the gate and into the alley. The brothers lived two houses down, Arturo three. Most of the houses didn't have fences and the boys ran shouting and laughing toward their homes, cutting past their neighbors backyards.

With a sigh, Josh shut the gate and locked it. His Paw Paw had built the fence when the neighbor kids had kept running through his garden. Now the garden and Paw Paw were gone, and Josh felt cut off from the rest of the world whenever he looked at the tall oak fence. He liked that. It was a good defense against zombies. Of course, all his Mom could talk about was how it made it safe for them to play outside.

Josh thought this was a joke. Just because they were living in a tiny town in the middle of Texas Hill Country, that didn't mean they were safe. He'd rather be living back at Fort Hood with all his old friends, surrounded by soldiers and their weapons. Instead they were living in Paw Paw and Mee Maw's old house, and it was so old the floors were kind of slanted. His Dad said it was because the house was settling. Josh was pretty sure it was going to fall apart. Or maybe that was just wishful thinking. Their old house in Killeen, Texas would have withstood a zombie assault for at least a few days.

With a sigh, he trudged across the spacious backyard toward the house painted in light blue with dark blue trim. Both the Texas and American flags hung on a flagpole just inside the fence in the sideyard. Paw Paw had been a patriot. He had been ecstatic when Jamie, Josh's dad, had enrolled in the Marines. He'd been in the Marines during the Vietnam War and had been very proud of his service. When he had died, Josh had been impressed by his burial. An honor guard had attended the funeral and had presented Mee Maw with the flag that had been draped over his casket. It wasn't until later, when his Dad had been in Iraq, that he had understood the significance of the flag and his great-grandmother's tears.

The screen door swung open and his mom stared down at him. "Stop dawdling."

"I'm not dawdling, Mom."

"You're dragging in here because you know you're in trouble."

"I didn't do anything," Josh answered defensively. He yanked off his cap as he entered the laundry room that led into the kitchen at the back of the house.

The delicious aroma of simmering chili mixed with the pungent smell of silver cleaner. An entire silver serving set was on the kitchen table, half of it polished to a brilliant shine, the other half grungy and mottled green. It reminded him of zombie skin. He had a feeling his mom was upset not because of

Drake acting like a brat, but because she was selling off family heirlooms again to pay the bills. Since Mee Maw and Paw Paw died within two months of each other, Josh knew that they were in a bad financial crisis. He hated it.

"That's right. You didn't do anything to keep your brother entertained while I cooked dinner and tried to get this stuff ready to mail off to that lady who bought it on eBay. I told you I have to get this done." His mother swept her hair out of her face, her huge blue eyes glimmering with tears.

A cool breeze was wafting through the open windows, but it was still humid in the kitchen from the cooking chili. His mother looked flushed, and, though he had denied it to his friends, his mom really was pretty.

Drake sat in the middle of the kitchen floor slamming his toy trucks together into a violent crash over and over again. His blond curls and rosy cheeks made him look like one of those baby angels, but Josh knew better. His brother was annoying and a devil. As if on cue, Drake looked up at him and gave him a huge smile.

"We were zombie training, Mom. I told you that. I'm trying to get everyone ready for when they come."

His mom didn't answer him. She just stood with her hands on her hips, staring down at him with a tired expression on her face.

"Seriously, Mom. On the forum last night, there was this story about a guy in San Antonio that the cops reported as dead. And they called in the coroner, but by the time he got there, the cops said the guy was alive, but incoherent. Out of control. And then nothing. A zombie, Mom. A zombie." Josh tried to make his voice as strong and firm as possible.

Sighing, his mother motioned toward Drake. "Take him into the living room and put on a movie. Not one of your movies, but one of his. I can't stand another night of him waking up and telling me that Paw Paw is trying to eat him."

Josh did feel bad about that and he felt his anger oozing away. He hated seeing his Mom look sad.

He thought that would be over once his father had returned from Iraq. But then Paw Paw had died, and once Mee Maw died, it just seemed to stay bad.

"Okay, Mom," he said quietly, then threw his arms around her waist.

Her body relaxed as she leaned over him, crushing him against her chest, and kissing his forehead. "I love you, Josh. I'm sorry to snap at you, but I gotta get this done."

"It's okay, Mom. I'll take better care of Drake. Even if he is annoying."

"Thanks, Josh," his mom said gratefully. She sat back down at the table and reached for a cleaning rag.

"C'mon, shorty. Let's go watch *Shrek*."

"I want to see Buzz Lightyear."

"Okay, whatever." Josh pushed the heavy wood door to the dining room open and Drake stomped past him, clutching his trucks to his chest.

"Turd head," Drake whispered, an evil little grin on his cute face.

Resisting the urge to hit him, Josh followed.

CHAPTER 2

Josh shoved Drake onto the couch along with his battered, stuffed dinosaur and turned on the TV. He ignored Drake as the toddler kept changing his mind as to which movie he wanted to watch and shoved the old videotape of *Shrek* into the ancient VCR. Most of Drake's moves had been bought at a second hand store in Killeen and his parents couldn't afford to buy new versions on DVD. Considering how rough Drake was with the tapes, it was probably a good idea to have them in the outdated VHS format. Most of Josh's zombie movies were second hand, too, but he had managed to get them on DVD. They were carefully stored in his room far away from his annoying brother.

"Watch this and shut up," Josh ordered.

"I'm gonna tell Mommy you're mean."

"What else is new?" Josh threw himself onto the loveseat beside the school bag he had discarded earlier when he had come home from school. Grabbing it up, he pulled out a battered copy of a zombie book he had found at a garage sale. The cover had lots of zombies. He wished it wasn't so wrinkled and stained. With a sigh, he opened it and started to read. Homework was for after dinner, when his mom and dad could help him.

Drake squirmed around on the couch, trying to get comfortable, dragging Rex, his stuffed dinosaur, around with him. Josh sighed and ignored him. He resented having to babysit his younger brother, but knew his mother and father needed him. Being the oldest child had its perks, but dealing with Drake was a real pain. He had wanted a brother so badly for so long. He never dreamed he would resent the very thing he had desired.

"I don't like this movie."

"Yes, you do."

"No."

"Yes."

"I want to see *Transformers*."

"Dad says you're too young and it will give you nightmares."

"I hate you."

Josh sighed and tried to read his book. He was just getting into the story when the book was pushed downward and Drake's cherubic face came into view. His chubby hand was bending the cover. Frustrated, Josh gave him a light shove.

"Lay off!"

"I want to see Transformers!"

"Dad said no!" Josh frowned as he raised the book. "Now shut up."

"You're mean," Drake pouted. "Rex is gonna eat you."

"Well, I hope zombies eat you," Josh responded

scornfully.

The scared look on his younger brother's face made him feel even guiltier, but Josh was too far into his bad mood to do anything more than raise his book and continue to read. Looking close to tears, Drake hurled the dinosaur onto the sofa and crawled up next to it. Stuffing his fingers in his mouth, he stared at the TV.

Josh tried to concentrate on the text, but he kept losing his train of thought. He began to feel bad for his behavior, but anger had a good grip on him. It wasn't his fault that his Dad didn't have a good job or that his grandparents had been stupid. He resented that he had to babysit Drake and pretend everything was okay as his Mom sold off family heirlooms and his Dad paced the creaky wood floors late at night.

The doorbell startled him and he tossed the book aside. "I'll get it, Mom!"

"Thanks, honey," her voice answered faintly from the kitchen.

Drake continued to stare at the TV, sucking

loudly on his fingers. His silence was accusing and terrible.

Ignoring him, Josh hurried to the door and yanked it open.

Corina, the love of his young life, stood on the doorstep. Three inches taller than him with long chestnut hair and clear gray eyes, she stared down at him through her glasses. One hand set on her hip, the other clutching a wad of dollar bills, she looked as annoyed as he had felt just a few seconds earlier.

"Hi," Josh managed.

"My mom said to bring this over to give to your mom. It's for some lame quilt or something," Corina drawled.

Pushing the screen door open, Josh reached out for the money. "Okay, I'll give it to her."

"Don't spend it on lame zombie stuff, okay?"

Josh could feel his face flushing and he had trouble finding his voice.

"Josh wants zombies to eat me," Drake said from beside him.

"I...uh...err..." Josh mumbled as his fingers

gripped the roll of dollar bills. For a second, he could feel her soft skin and the tips of her sharp nails.

Corina let go of the money abruptly, as if knowing he was relishing his brief moment of touching her hand, and dropped to her knees. “He did! That’s so mean! Josh, you’re a meanie!”

Drake threw his arms around Corina’s neck and sobbed softly against her. “He is a big meanie.”

As he always did when around Corina, Josh lost his voice and senses. He could only stare at her and wonder if she would wait for him to grow a few inches taller and a few years older so he could ask her out. She was two years older, but it felt like a million. She was the forbidden older woman, the love of his short life, and he felt stupid whenever she looked at him. Of course, this was only made worse by the fact she had been his and Drake’s babysitter before his parents decided he was old enough to take care of Drake.

Ruffling Drake’s blond curls, Corina kissed his brow. “It’s okay, Drake. Zombies aren’t real. But if they were, they would eat Josh for being a meanie."

"Actually, they would just eat me for being...uh...meat." Josh faltered as his eyes trailed to her neckline. He could see down her shirt. Her small breasts were tucked into a pink bra.

Noticing his gaze, Corina stood up, holding Drake, and gave Josh her darkest look. "Well, Drake has immunity to zombies, so they're going to eat you. Right, Drake?"

"Right!"

"That's not how it works," Josh began to protest. "Zombies eat because-"

"Your brother is a nerd," Corina said, smiling at Drake.

With a sigh, Josh shoved the money into his pocket.

"Yeah!" Drake looked pleased and snuggled into Corina's arms.

"Make sure your mom gets that, okay? Cause my mom will kick my butt if you don't." Kissing Drake's cheek, she set him down.

"Yeah, I will. Promise."

"You guys really moving away?" Corina pushed her glasses up on her nose.

"My dad is going to go to Austin and try to become a police officer there. So, yeah, we might move away."

"Austin is cool," Corina assured him. "But it will suck to see you move away."

Josh tried not to smile too wide at her comment. "Yeah, well, you know there is, like, the internet and stuff to talk."

"Yeah. I'm sure the Cowboy brothers will keep in touch and stuff with you."

"My screen name is "livingdeadboy," no spaces." Josh tried to sound casual, but he was sure he sounded desperate.

Corina just smiled and kissed Drake on the cheek again. "Hope your dad gets the job. This town sucks anyway." She hopped off the porch and headed back to her home next door.

"She's my girlfriend," Drake informed Josh, shoving past him.

"Whatever, shrimp," Josh answered, closing the

screen door slowly. He tried to keep an eye on his beloved until she disappeared into her house. With a sigh, he shut the door.

CHAPTER 3

Deeply engrossed in his book, Josh didn't hear the front door open. He was so completely enmeshed in the world of the shambling undead that when his dad's rough hand touched his cheek, he jumped with a yelp.

Drake burst into laughter, dangling from their father's forearm. He was hanging there like a monkey, swinging back and forth, oblivious to the exhaustion etched in his parent's face.

"Kinda deep into that book, huh?"

Josh could feel his cheeks reddening as he shoved the book into his backpack. "Yeah. It was a good part, too. The zombies were just about to eat the policeman."

"Well, I'm rooting for the policeman to shoot them in the head," his dad answered with a wry smile.

"In da head," Drake said gleefully.

Josh shoved his hair out of his eyes and slid off the loveseat to hug his dad. James Rondell, known as Jamie to his friends, smelled like sweat and his blue Walmart vest was rumpled from his long day. Drake looked like their mom, but Josh definitely looked like his dad. They both had sandy hair and green eyes. His dad's eyes had fine lines reaching toward his hairline and dark circles underneath. Though he was twelve, Josh still felt young enough to kiss his dad's cheek and he pressed his lips against the dry, rough skin.

"Did you have a good day at school?"

"I got an A in spelling."

"That's my boy."

"I can't spell," Drake chirped.

"That's because you are three," Jamie answered with a grin.

Lynette shoved open the door from the kitchen. "Good! You're home. Now we can eat!"

Josh let go of his dad and watched him stroll over to his mom. He hated when his parents got mushy, but lately they had been fighting so much he needed the reassurance that their kiss gave him. Drake tagged along behind Jamie and tried to push his way between his parents' knees. Josh felt like clocking him. Last night the fight had been really bad and he was relieved to see his dad kiss his mom firmly on the mouth then hold her close for a few seconds.

"I'm hungry!" Drake wailed.

"Josh, get the table set. Drake, go wash your hands with Daddy."

"I'm hungry!"

"I know, buddy. Let's go get those hands washed." Jamie lifted Drake over his shoulder and headed toward the downstairs bathroom.

Sighing, Josh pulled open his grandmother's old china cabinet and began to pull out bowls for the chili. Growing up had its perks, but he sometimes resented that Drake got so much attention. The older he got the more work he had to do around the house while Drake was able to run around and be annoying.

His mom shoved the kitchen door open with her hip, swiveled on one foot, and managed to make it to the table without spilling the big pot of chili. Setting it down on a hot pan holder in the center of the table, she let out a groan.

"I think I made too much."

The china bowls clicked against the table as he set them down. He winced, trying to be careful, but his Mom was too distracted staring at the big pot to give him any attention.

"What is it, Mom?"

"I just keep forgetting I'm not cooking for six anymore." She shook her head, her blond hair shimmering around her face as it shifted under the light from the small chandelier.

Josh looked down at the six spoons he had clutched in one hand. His grandparents had died so fast and so close to one another it still didn't feel real. He kept expecting to see both of them wandering through the old house. He quickly laid down the spoons and returned the extras to the drawer of the sideboard.

The kitchen door whooshed shut behind his mother as he began to fold the linen napkins. Back in Killeen, they had eaten out of plastic bowls with old mismatched spoons and paper napkins. But once they moved in with his grandparents, his mom had adopted his grandmother's routine for dinner. Josh kind of liked it.

Returning to the table, his mother set a basket of corn muffins next to the chili. Steam rose off the freshly baked bread, making Josh's stomach grumble with hunger.

Drake and Jamie returned to the dining room, laughing about something they had shared. Hoisting Drake onto his chair with the bumper seat, Jamie looked more relaxed than Josh had seen him in awhile. Josh quickly finished setting out the three glasses and Drake's plastic cup and took his seat.

"Now, the chili may be a little hot. I think I may have over killed just a little because I got distracted," Lynette confessed as she poured ice water from the big pitcher.

"I like it hot," Jamie assured her. "Nothing like your tongue on fire to let you know you're eating real Texas chili."

"I like it hot, too, Daddy!"

Josh rolled his eyes at his younger brother.

"Josh, go turn off the TV," his mom ordered, taking her place at the table.

With a sigh, he slid off his chair and hurried into the living room. He grabbed up the remote, turned off the movie, and hit the eject button. The tape slid out with a loud clunk and the TV immediately switched to the broadcast channel.

"...as the riots continue. Authorities continue to remain silent as to whether or not the violence is being spurred on by a terrorist attack. Several anonymous sources from deep within the FBI claim that they have heard that terrorist cells may have spiked the water supply with a drug that causes the extreme violent behavior we have been witnessing in New York, Chicago, Los Angeles and Atlanta. All flights into those cities have been canceled as pockets of violence continue to erupt on the streets. The President has released a statement that defends his move to declare those cities quarantined. Troops began arriving..."

Josh stood mesmerized as helicopters hovered over the cities, camera crews filming the bloody rioters below them. It was violent and surreal. It looked like a zombie movie.

"Josh, hurry up! The food is getting cold."

"But, Mom, I think there is something bad going on. It might be zombies!"

"Josh, obey your mother. Turn off the TV," his father called out.

"Dad! Seriously! Zombies!" Josh looked at the news coverage again. A bunch of crazed people were hurling themselves against the doors of the CNN Center in Atlanta. They were covered in blood.

"Josh! Get in here! Now!" His dad's voice was firm.

"Gosh!" Josh turned off the TV and stomped back into the dining room. "Seriously, those people rioting were covered in blood-"

"That's enough of that," his mother said firmly. "We're eating now. Sit down."

"Sick of seeing the footage of all that," Jamie groused, serving Drake some chili.

"I just hope this doesn't start up the war again," his wife sighed.

"If it is terrorists, who knows what will happen. Two days of this shi-stuff is ridiculous. They should just round up the troublemakers and lock them up until they figure out what is wrong with them."

"I heard on NPR that the media is blowing it out of proportion. That it's really very isolated."

"They were covered in blood, Mom. It's not a good thing if you got people attacking other people covered in blood. It's zombies!" Josh stared at the chili his father served him. "Zombies, okay?"

His mother looked at his dad, imploring him to

get Josh off the zombie thing. It was the same look she always got when she felt Josh was obsessing.

"There is no such thing as zombies, Josh. But there is such thing as bio-terrorism. That's what we're dealing with most likely. That, or some really bad drugs ended up on the street."

"Drugs are bad," Drake decided. He was munching on some cornbread. His face and hands were coated in crumbs.

Josh stabbed at his chili with his spoon, a frown etched on his forehead. His stomach clenched and his throat felt constricted. "What if it's zombies and you're away in Austin and they come here?"

"Enough talk about zombies. You're scaring your brother," Lynette said sharply, her blue eyes reflecting her displeasure.

"Let's say grace," Jamie said after a short, tense moment.

Josh took his mother's hand on his right, and his Dad's on his left. Both parents leaned over the table to grab hold of Drake's crumb-covered little hands. The golden head bowed, surprisingly reverently, and Josh followed suit. He felt grumpy and scared. He hoped God didn't notice.

"Dear heavenly Father, bless this meal we are about to eat. Bless my wife for making it and bless my children who eat it. Remind us to keep our faith even when times are hard and that you are always with us, even when we are afraid. In the name of your son, Jesus, Amen." Jamie squeezed Josh's hand gently, then let go. "Let's dig in!"

"Does Jesus like chili?" Drake asked as he tried to shove more cornbread into his mouth.

"If Jesus were here, he would love your mom's chili," Jamie answered with a grin. "Wouldn't he, Josh?"

"I guess," Josh grumbled. His stomach hurt and it was hard to swallow. He hated that his parents weren't paying attention to him. What he had seen on TV had looked just like a zombie movie. Why couldn't they see that? Why couldn't the newscasters, soldiers and president see that?

Lynette sighed as she buttered a piece of cornbread. "Your dad is leaving tomorrow for

Austin for almost a whole week. Let's try and make this a good dinner, okay?"

Nodding, Josh took a bite of the chili. It tasted good, but it was hard to swallow.

"If I get the job in Austin, a lot of things will change for the better," his dad said.

"I know." Gulping down his water, Josh felt his throat open a little. His fear was still pulsating in his head, but he knew no one was going to listen to him.

Reluctantly, he forced himself to eat and listen to his parents chatter on about the possibility of a new job and new home in Austin. Soon they were laughing as they made plans, sharing their hopes and dreams, as Drake rambled on occasionally about something that really didn't make sense. Josh didn't want to sit and listen to his folks. He wanted to rush into the living room and turn on the TV to watch the news. He wanted to turn on the family computer and check out the zombie forums.

Instead, he ate slowly, contributing very little to the family conversation, until at last he was excused to do his homework. As he set his bowl in the kitchen sink, he looked out the window at the last remnants of the setting Texas sun. It was beautiful, but the darkness falling over his neighborhood made him shiver.

CHAPTER 4

The boughs of the big tree creaked and moaned as the night breeze twisted through its leaves like rushing water. The soft wind tumbled through the open window of the tree house and rustled Josh's hair. The boy was reading his zombie book again and making notes in a notebook he had covered in zombie pictures. It was his guide to all things zombie and he had made it himself. His homework was done and he had thirty minutes to himself before he had to go upstairs to bed. A flashlight resting on a shelf over his shoulder illuminated the words on the page.

Shivering, Josh zipped his hoodie all the way up to his neck and nestled down in the old pillows and quilts his mother had let him take up into the tree house. The zombie book didn't really have any new methods for killing the undead, but it did make his skin crawl. He hoped and prayed that his parents were right and that the crazed people in those cities were just victims of a terrorist attack.

"Josh?" His father's voice called out to him from below.

"Yeah, Dad?"

"I'm coming up."

"Okay." Josh carefully set his *Dawn of the Dead* bookmark he had made himself between the pages of the book and closed it.

He could hear his dad grunting as he climbed up the makeshift ladder made out of boards nailed into the trunk of the tree. Jamie finally reached the doorway and lugged himself inside. The tree house was big enough to sit maybe four adults. They wouldn't be able to stand up, just stoop over, but it was perfect for kids. Posters were taped to the walls, shelves his dad had built were loaded up with toys, and a cooler tucked into one corner was filled with water bottles. There was a large nook in the trunk the tree house was built around and it was filled with cans of ravioli, chips, cookies, and other food the kids stashed up there. Josh called it emergency rations. The tree house was tucked up against the trunk of the tree and securely built along the thickest branches. It had an odd, almost wobbly look to it, but it was very sturdy.

His dad settled on a large pillow one of the other kids in the Zombie Hunters had brought from home, looking around at the interior of the tree house "We did a very good job, didn't we?"

"Yeah. It's cool."

Jamie stared down into the yard, his expression thoughtful. Josh thought it looked like his dad was weighing something in his mind.

"I won't be here when you get up in the morning. I need to get an early start to Austin. I just wanted to ask you to do a few things for me when I'm gone, okay?"

Josh nodded as he sat up and scooted over to sit next to his dad.

"I need you to help your mom out-"

"Dad, I do! But Drake-"

"Now, listen, Josh. Calm down. Okay?"

"Yeah."

Jamie slung his arm around Josh's shoulders and tugged him closer. "Things are really rough right now for all of us. None of this is easy on any of us and sometimes your mom and I get so caught up in what we are doing, we forget about your needs, too. You're eleven..."

"Twelve. I just had my birthday last month."

"Twelve. That's right. Man, you're growing older by the second."

"Yeah, I know." Josh nodded his head, feeling the weight of his years on his shoulders along with his father's arm.

"So, you're twelve, and you got your own thing going on with your friends, this tree house, your zombie obsession-"

"Zombies could be real, Dad."

Jamie sighed. "There are worse things out there than zombies, Josh. And I've seen it. Maybe its easier for you to be afraid of zombies instead of moving away to a new city and leaving your friends, I don't know. But you need to drop it while I'm gone. Your mom is really nervous about how things are right now in this family. She just lost her grandparents who raised her and she's going to lose her family home. Yeah, it ain't much. This tree house will probably outlive it -"

Josh grinned at that. His headquarters was awesome.

"- but your mom is having a rough time. She needs you to help her get through all of this."

"Dad, I do everything she tells me to!"

"Yeah, you do, and I appreciate it. But she'll need you to help her without her asking you constantly. Just get in there and help with Drake more and that will help her out a lot."

His dad ruffled his hair affectionately as Josh

sighed. He knew his surly attitude didn't help. Often, it just made his parents cranky at him.

"Think you can do that and tone down the zombie stuff?"

"Yeah, yeah. But, Dad, those people on the news, they looked like zombies!"

"I was just watching MSNBC and they are saying it is some sort of terrorist attack. They put some sort of drug in the water that makes people violent. The army has it under control. They are suggesting we all drink bottled water until the crisis is over. It's going to be okay, Josh. I wouldn't be leaving for Austin if I didn't believe it is going to be okay. I know it seems close to us, but that's the thing about the news. It makes the world feel much smaller than it actually is. Besides, your mother can shoot the wings off a fly. If there were zombies, they'd be headless if they came near your mom."

Josh rubbed his nose and looked toward the house. It was mostly dark now. He supposed Drake was asleep.

"Your mom has a job as a substitute teacher at

your school tomorrow, so she'll need you to help out with Drake in the morning since she'll be getting ready for work."

"Okay."

"On Sunday, make sure you help her get Drake calmed down and into his church clothes. There is going to be a social afterward, so help keep Drake distracted while she makes pies."

"Okay."

"And let Drake play with you and your friends so she can deal with packing up our stuff without him bothering her."

Josh started to protest, but changed his mind. "Fine, Dad."

His dad pressed a firm kiss to his forehead. "Thank you, Josh. I know it was rough on you when I was away during the war, but you're a good kid and I have faith in you to help your mom and brother when I'm not here. You have always been a good kid."

That brought a grin to his face. "Well, I am a cool kid."

"Yes, you are. Now, let's get back into the house and to bed. We all have a long day tomorrow."

Josh grabbed his book and notebook and tossed them into the wire basket dangling on a thick rope that was pulled taunt between the tree house and a pulley outside his bedroom window. His dad had put up the rope and pulley system to keep Josh from falling when trying to carry things up and down from the tree house Josh pulled on the thick line and the basket drifted over the backyard and right up to the window.

Following his father down the ladder, Josh felt a little better than he had before. Jamie had a soothing voice and a way of making him feel more confident and safe. With his beard and long bangs, Jamie didn't look much like a solider anymore, but his arms were strong and his gaze steady. Josh never wanted to see his dad disappointed in him. Despite his annoyance at his little brother and the circumstances of his life, he would do his best to do what his dad asked.

Together, they walked toward the house, his

dad's big hand a comforting presence on his shoulder.

CHAPTER 5

It was the voices that drew him out of his sleep. Josh rolled over in his bed, groggily dragging his covers over his body.

“It will be okay, won’t it?” his mother’s voice whispered.

The creak of the floorboards outside his door and the gentle thump of what was probably his dad’s suitcase being set down drew him further into the waking world. The digital clock on his bed stand read 5:30 AM in bright blue numbers.

"It will be. I promise. We're done in this town, Lynette. There are no real jobs here and this house was willed to your church. I'm not sure why your granddaddy decided to do that, but we have to move on."

"I know. I just...I really want you to get this job."

"It'll work out, we'll move to Austin, and the boys will have a better life. C'mon. Let's go downstairs before we wake the boys."

Their footsteps were soft on the wood floor and finally faded away as they went downstairs. Josh stared into the darkness around his bed, trying not to think of the terrible images on TV or the zombies from his nightmares. He had to trust what his dad said was true and do as he had asked. Though it would be hard, he would take care of his younger brother and help his mom out more. He'd do his best to take care of them until his dad got back from Austin. Hopefully by then, whatever the terrorists had done would be over with and the sick feeling in his stomach would go away.

CHAPTER 6

"Your dad is so much cooler than our dad," Roger decided as the boys trudged up the sidewalk from the cafeteria to the main school building. "First he was a soldier and now he is going to be a policeman."

Sucking nosily on his grape Popsicle, Troy nodded his head in agreement. "Totally, so much cooler. Our dad is the lame ol' school counselor."

"I like Austin," Arturo decided, rummaging around in the bottom of the small chocolate chip cookie bag his mom had put in his lunch. "It's neat. I like to go to the UT football games with my dad there even if I have to put up with my stepbrother."

Josh shrugged his shoulder under the straps of his backpack and tucked his hands into his jean pockets. "My dad is cool, but he makes me scared that I'm gonna let him down."

"Just don't beat Drake's butt into the ground and he won't kick yours when he gets back," Arturo decided with a wide grin.

"Don't worry. As annoying as Drake can be sometimes, I promised my dad I would help my mom and I will. It's just laying low on the zombie stuff that is going to be super-hard."

"Yeah, especially with those crazy, scary people on TV," Arturo agreed. "My mom won't even let me watch the news right now."

"It's terrorists," Troy asserted. "Not zombies."

"I wish it was zombies," Roger decided, pulling his Dallas Cowboy cap over his black hair. "Then I wouldn't have to do that stupid math test."

"I hate math," Josh agreed. "Almost as much as

running zombies."

Roger and Troy had skipped two grades and were in the 6th grade with Josh and Arturo. They had been home-schooled for several years before their dad had found a job as the school counselor. The other sixth graders avoided the boys, but Josh and Arturo liked them. The boys were also neighbors, so it made it easier to all hang out.

"Running zombies suck," Troy agreed. "Let's watch the rest of that zombie movie."

The boys gathered around a bench, Troy still eating his Popsicle. Arturo tossed his dessert bag away as Roger sprawled onto the bench looking bored. Josh sat down and pulled out his iPod. He loaded up the zombie movie they had been watching the day before and the boys gathered around to watch.

The sun was blazing overhead, but the breeze was cool. The school was an old, beige brick building surrounded by a dozen portable buildings. The cafeteria was connected to the school by a covered walkway, but most of the kids hung out around the benches scattered between the two structures. The grass was slowly turning from brown to green as spring took hold, but there were bare patches around the benches and trees where the kids loitered, waiting for class to being again.

Kindergarten to eighth grade were stuffed into the school. The high school kids were in another building across the street. It was newer and nicer. The two schools sat on the edge of town near the highway, old farmhouses and a few fields separating them from the main neighborhood and downtown area.

"What a bunch of losers," a voice taunted them.

Josh looked up from the zombie mayhem to see Sam Pickett standing over them. He was the sheriff's son and the resident school outcast. He was big, ruddy-faced, and strawberry blond. Because of the extra weight and his big double chin, his face looked like it was tucked into a flesh-colored box.

"Loooserrrrrrrs," Sam drawled out.

Sighing, Josh turned off the movie. "What do

you want, lame-o?"

"Looooooooooooooosssssssssssssseeeeeeeeeeee eeeersssssssssss," Sam said again, dragging the word out as long and loud as he could.

The four friends just stared at him, waiting for him to make a move. After a year of Sam following them around and bugging them, they knew his usual routine by heart. He would try to bully them, then beg them to be his friend. It was pretty pathetic.

"What are you watchin'? Huh? Watching stupid zombie movies? Huh? Zombies are dumb. They're lame. Jason is cooler."

"Jason is a zombie," Roger said, annoyed.

"And he's a dumb zombie," Troy continued. "Because he doesn't eat what he kills."

"Therefore, he is lame," Arturo added.

Sam stared at them, processing this information. "Let me in your club."

"No," Josh said firmly.

"C'mon. I'm cool."

"No, you're not." Arturo shook his head. "You

are, in fact, the very definition of uncool."

Sam frowned, deep lines forming on his huge forehead. "My dad is the sheriff."

"That makes you double uncool," Josh answered.

"Let me in. I like zombies."

"You just said they're not cool," Troy reminded him.

"Uh, I was just teasing you," Sam answered, tugging nervously on his bottom lip with his teeth.

"What is your favorite zombie movie?" Josh asked, lifting his eyebrows and folding his arms.

"Uh, the one with the zombie that eats that guy," Sam faltered.

"That is like every zombie movie known to man," Arturo said with disgust.

"Uh, the one with the army guys," Sam persisted.

"Which one?" Josh raised his brows higher.

"Uh..."

Arturo pointed at Roger. "Favorite zombie movie with soldiers!"

"*Day of the Dead*. The original!"

Arturo gave Sam a long, dark look. "It's not that

hard, turd head."

"My dad doesn't let me watch zombie movies! Okay!" Sam's face was growing redder. It looked almost like a blotchy tomato.

"Lame," Roger decided, scrunching up his face. "Real lame."

Sliding to his feet, Josh gazed at Sam steadily. "Look, tard-o, learn something about zombies and maybe, just maybe, we might let you hang with us."

"We can use him as zombie bait," Troy decided. "He's so fat, they'd get him first."

Sam's eyes were watery, either from unshed tears or the harsh wind blowing across the lawn. "They would not!"

"Uh huh!" Arturo decided.

"My dad has a gun! He's the sheriff!"

Josh's gaze was stolen away by a motorcycle drawing up the curving driveway to the school. It was Brad Cooper and Corina was holding onto his waist for dear life as he guided the big, grumbling bike up to the sidewalk. Dressed in blue leggings, cowboy boots, a short skirt and denim jacket,

Corina was breathtakingly beautiful as always. Her long hair was tucked into two long ponytails that hung over her shoulders and she shoved her glasses up her pert nose as the motorcycle came to a stop. Brad, tall, blond, and good-looking, grinned at her as she slid off his bike.

"Dude, there is no way you can steal her away from that guy," Roger declared.

"He's got a motorcycle, muscles and is on the high school baseball team. You're so screwed," Arturo agreed.

"Shut up," Josh said automatically. He tried not to watch as Brad kissed Corina's cheek and clung to her hand.

Sam's eyes slowly widened. "You like Corina? Wow. She is like so pretty and smart and older and—"

"Shut up, Sam," Josh said sharply.

Corina pulled her hand away and started walking toward the school.

Glancing down at his watch, Josh saw that the lunch period was almost over. His nerves were getting the best of him again. Not only was his dad away in Austin, the terrorists making people crazy, his math test about to happen in ten minutes, but Corina was dating an older, better looking man.

"She's hot," Roger decided.

"Though Josh's mom is way hotter," Troy added.

"Shut it, Troy," Josh ordered.

Corina drew nearer as Brad sped off on his motorcycle, Josh felt the knot in his stomach clench tighter. Nothing about this day felt right. He ran his hand through his sandy hair as he looked away from Corina as she approached. Trying to look as nonchalant as possible, he turned toward Sam.

"Just don't say anything embarrassing to her, okay?"

Sam screwed up his mouth thoughtfully. "Let me into your club."

"You're gonna blackmail me?"

"Uh huh."

"Dude, that is way lame," Arturo decided.

"I want into the club," Sam repeated.

Corina was drawing closer and Josh did not feel

like having Sam blathering not only to her, but the whole school about his crush. This was the last thing he needed on top of all the other crap.

"Okay, fine. Don't tell Corina and we'll let you take a zombie test to get in. But you have to watch *Night of the Living Dead*," Josh said in an urgent tone. "We'll ask you questions about it and you have to answer all of them, okay?"

Sam was so excited by the prospect; he was breathing hard and could only nod his head.

"Do we have to do that?" Troy protested.

"Yeah, do we have to do that? C'mon everyone knows you have a crush on her." Roger looked sullen as he glared at Sam.

"Plus he's a retard," Arturo added. "A total retard."

"You're not supposed to say retard," Troy corrected. "It's a slur. Like the "n" word."

"C'mon, guys. I'm the leader, so a test." Josh turned back to Sam. "Okay?"

Sam continued to nod his head as Corina strolled past them. The boys all watched her go by, her long hair rippling in the breeze.

"Hi, Corina," Josh managed to say.

"Hi," she answered just before she was mobbed by her two best friends.

"Did you go to Subway with him?"

"Did he kiss you?"

"He's so totally hot!"

"Oh, my gawd, Corina!"

The girls hurried off, giggling and talking rapidly to each other leaving Josh staring after Corina once again. The warning bell rang. The 6th, 7th, and 8th graders began to trudge inside, regretfully leaving the oasis of their lunch period behind to face the horrors of math, English, and history for the rest of the day. The younger children had already had lunch earlier and Josh saw the kitchen crews mopping the floors inside the cafeteria. As he joined the throng outside the double doors to go inside, he glanced over at the field behind the school that gradually dipped down to the highway below. The wind was loud as it rushed over the field and wove around the school. He could barely hear the sound of the cars rushing toward unknown destinations on the highway nearby.

"I hate math," Arturo muttered beside him. "I hate it."

"Do you hear sirens?" Josh strained, trying to hear what the wind was trying to snatch away.

"Nope. And, I still hate math."

The kids jostled each other as they pushed inside the building. Josh got squished between Sam and Arturo. He let the stream of kids carry him toward the doors, shuffling his feet to the slow pace. Glancing over his shoulder, he hoped to see Corina, but instead caught sight of a lone figure stumbling to the top of the hill in the distance.

Zombie!

The crowd of kids poured into the hallway and Josh was swept along with them. He tried to turn back, but some bigger kids shoved him along. Finally, he managed to get past the largest cluster of kids that reeked of sweat and food, and rushed out the doors just before they closed. He looked to the spot where the person had come over the top of the hill, but there was no sign of the figure now. Now the only movement in the area was the gentle swaying of the trees in the wind.

"Get inside! Lunch is over! The bell is about to ring!" The big booming voice was that of the assistant principal. He was a former football player and huge. Other than Troy, he was the only black person in town. His wife and step-children were Mexican-American and sometimes people thought Troy was his.

"Mr. Johnson, I saw someone over there. They were stumbling and stuff like a zombie." Josh explained.

"There was an accident on the highway. Maybe it was someone trying to find help. I'll go check it out," Mr. Johnson answered.

"Sir, seriously. I think it may have really been a zombie," Josh persisted.

"Josh, I know you like zombies, but they aren't real. Now go get to class. You're going to be tardy." Mr. Johnson pushed the door open for him.

Reluctantly, Josh started inside, but then

stopped. “Be careful if you go over there. Please, Mr. Johnson.”

“I will. Now go!”

Josh watched the heavy orange door slam shut and scuffed his sneaker against the floor with irritation. No one ever listened to him.

The hallway was nearly empty. Only a few kids were left rushing to their classes, hall monitors shouting at them to slow down. Josh trudged to class, his sneakers squeaking against the floor as he dragged his feet.

Corina stepped out of the girls’ restroom and glanced toward him. He gave her an awkward smile as he passed her.

She gave him a small smile back.

His heart bursting with joy, he ducked into his class. Her smile almost forced the thought of that lonely figure standing on the edge of the school grounds from his mind.

“Put away all your books and notes. We’re starting the test,” his teacher, Mrs. Adkins ordered.

With groans, the class began to tuck away their

belongings. Josh shoved his backpack under his chair and as he raised his head, he saw Troy staring out the window. Turning around, he saw Mr. Johnson walking toward the edge of the school yard.

"What is he doing?" Troy wondered aloud.

The same staggering figure Josh had seen before stumbled out of a copse of trees and held out a hand toward Mr. Johnson.

The blinds were drawn abruptly shut.

"Pay attention to your test, Mr. Rondell," Mrs. Adkins said in a firm voice as she let go of the drawstring. She was short, pudgy, and had very short dark hair shot through with gray. She slapped the test down onto his desk and walked on. She continued to close all the blinds as she handed out the tests. "No more distractions, people. Concentrate on your test."

The room grew dimmer as the florescent lights buzzed and shimmered over their heads.

Fear gnawing at his stomach, Josh looked down at his test. He couldn't make sense of the figures on the page and he felt a terrible anticipation growing inside of him. It took him a few seconds to realize what he was waiting for.

He was waiting for screams.

CHAPTER 7

Thirty minutes later, Josh stared at his partially filled out test. None of it was making sense to him and he was writing down random numbers. An F seemed imminent, but he couldn't concentrate. The image of that lone figure kept playing over and over again in his mind.

The loudspeaker in the corner of the room suddenly buzzed to life, crackling and whining just a bit before Mr. Johnson's voice pushed through the static.

"This is not a test, ladies and gentleman. I need all of you to stand up and line up at your classroom doors this very moment. School is now closing and you will be leaving on the school buses. Even if your parents regularly pick you up, you must get on a bus. All the buses will be going to the same location and your parents will be notified."

Mrs. Adkins pointed at the door as the other kids slowly got to their feet. She snapped her fingers at Arturo to hurry him up. Josh quickly grabbed his backpack.

"What is going on?" a girl asked as she lined up.

"Shush," Mrs. Adkins answered.

"What is going on?" Troy whispered to Josh.

"I think it's zombies," Josh answered in a low voice.

For once Troy didn't roll his eyes. He had seen the strange figure in the trees, too.

"Nerds," one of the other kids hissed, shoving them from behind.

"You are to exit the front doors of the school in a fast, orderly fashion. Get immediately onto the first bus you see. Keep moving as fast as you can." Mr. Johnson continued as Josh realized how much he sounded out of breath. "Just keep moving no matter what you see."

"What does that mean?" Troy's eyes widened. "That doesn't sound good."

"Troy, keep it shut and line up," Mrs. Adkins ordered.

Despite the stern set of Mrs. Adkins jaw, Josh saw fear flicker in her eyes. She pushed the door open and motioned her class out into the already packed hallway. The younger classes had the kids walking with their hands on the shoulders of the person in front of them, while the lines of the older students soon disintegrated into a mob.

The teachers were motioning frantically to each other as they herded their classes toward the front of the school. Straining to see over the tops of the kids' heads, Josh looked around for his mom, who was subbing in the lower grades.

The screams began at the back of the crowd and spread like wildfire. Immediately, all the children began pushing toward the two sets of double doors at the front of the school. Some of the younger students began to sob in fear and the crush of bodies increased around Josh. He could barely move.

"What is going on, dude?" Roger grabbed hold of Josh's shirt, trying to keep close to him and Troy.

"We saw a zombie," Troy answered. "A real zombie."

"No way!"

"Way," Josh answered, trying to maneuver through the crowd.

The screaming was growing louder and it was hard to tell if it was from fear or something far worse. The tidal wave of children was chaotic with younger children being tossed into lockers as the older kids pushed ahead. Teachers shouted out orders that no one listened to as panic gripped the children. Over all the chaos, Mr. Johnson's voice continued to give directions over the loudspeaker that everyone disregarded.

For a brief moment, Josh caught sight of his

mom far ahead of him. Lynette was near the door, waving at him. Then there were more screams behind him and a giant surge from behind pushed him forward.

"Stop pushing! Stop pushing!"

Josh felt someone's elbow dig painfully into his ribs as another kid stepped on his feet.

More screams and another push knocked Josh off balance. He felt Arturo and Troy grab for him, but he fell into the lockers, sliding downward. A couple of 4th graders crashed into him sending him to the floor. Trying to get his hands under his body to push upwards, Josh began to panic. His backpack was wedged under the lockers, making it hard for him to get up. Sneakers, boots, and flats all stampeded past him as the panic swelled. The screams were nonstop and terror gripped Josh as he thought about what might be causing the terror.

What if the zombies were in the building?

"C'mon," a voice grunted as hands gripped his arm, tugging him upward.

He finally managed to get his knees under him

and pushed with his hands. Corina held onto his arm, looking at him worriedly.

"I got knocked down," he said, sounding painfully stupid and obvious. "Everyone went crazy."

"The boys in my class started growling and grabbing kids," she answered, dragging him along with her. "It freaked everyone out and the morons think it's funny."

The hall was nearly empty as the crowd moved onto the school's front lawn. Josh and Corina hurried behind the remains of the throng as the older boys jostled each other, laughing.

Josh adjusted his backpack and tried to catch his breath. He could feel fear coursing through his veins, making his heart beat faster and his breath come in short breaths.

"I thought something was behind us," he said finally, feeling foolish.

"It was just them being stupid," Corina said angrily. She let go of his arm, but stayed at his side.

Taking another deep breath, Josh let his shoulders relax. His imagination was running away with him. Something else had to be going on. It couldn't be zombies, could it?

Josh looked over his shoulder toward the doors at the far end of the main hall that opened to the courtyard and cafeteria. His breath caught in his throat as he saw the dark shape of a person pressed up against the glass inset in the door. It was pounding on the window with one hand.

"Corina," he gasped.

She turned, looked down the hall, and then back at him. "What?"

"I think..."

"It's not a zombie, Josh. It's probably one of the stupid kids goofing off." She looked cross, but uneasy.

Now that the hall was almost empty, they could hear the steady banging echoing down the corridor. Another shape appeared at the other door. It, too, began to bang on the door.

"Let's get out of here," she said, her voice suddenly sounding afraid.

Corina grabbed Josh's hand and together they

ran toward the front doors. As they passed the front office, Josh caught sight of Mr. Johnson in the main office near the P.A. System. His shirt was covered in blood and Miss Thomas was trying to bandage his shoulder and arm. Roger and Troy's dad, Mr. Inmon, was also in the office, talking quickly on the phone. He was a slight man with thin brown hair and a small mustache and as he talked, his hand shook. Mr. Inmon noticed Josh and urgently motioned him toward the door.

"Get out there, Josh! Get on the bus!"

Corina shoved the door open to the outside world and they were temporarily blinded by the afternoon sun. As Josh's eyes adjusted, he took in the chaos enveloping the school parking lot as the screams, shouts, and honking horns deafened him.

"This is bad," Corina said.

"Yeah," Josh answered. "Really, really bad."

CHAPTER 8

Teachers and students were clustered near the bus lane. The dingy yellow buses were lined up in a long line next to the curb, engines rumbling. Coaches and teachers frantically pushed kids up into the buses as sirens sounded from the direction of the highway. Some of the younger children cried while the older kids joked and shoved each other around. Over the loudspeaker, Mr. Johnson's voice continued to breathlessly order everyone onto the buses.

The cars and trucks pulling up to the school at terrifying speeds caused the most commotion and panic. Parents slammed on their brakes, leaped out of their vehicles, and plunged into the crowd of children, screaming out their offspring's name.

"What is going on?" Corina exclaimed as two trucks almost crashed as they pulled into the bus lane at the same time, blocking a bus that was trying to depart.

"People are freaking out, that's what!" Josh looked around desperately for his mom. "We need to get out of here before it gets worse. Before Mr. Johnson becomes a zombie!"

"There are no such things as-"

A bus roared over the curb, edging around the trucks blocking it as several parents beat on the side of it, screaming for their kids. Teachers pushed the students back from the departing bus as more cars poured into the school complex. People drove up onto the lawn, disregarding the parking lot or bus lane and ran toward the children. Josh watched several parents shove other kids aside to grab their own. As people panicked, the situation grew increasingly dangerous.

Troy, Roger and Arturo ran up to Josh, Sam trailing behind. The bigger boy was huffing and puffing, fear etched on his face.

"Dude, it's zombies," Troy exclaimed, breathing heavily. "I heard one of the teachers telling Coach Ray that there was an accident on the highway and those crazed people were attacking the police and the ambulance guys. It's less than a mile from here, dude."

"They're not real zombies. They're infected," Roger corrected his brother.

"Totally *28 Days Later*, not *Night of the Living Dead*," Arturo agreed.

"They'll kill us just the same," Troy answered grimly.

They all fell silent, then Corina took a deep breath and shouted, "What is going on?"

"Crazy people coming to kill us!" Sam yelled at her. "Aren't you listening? Are you retarded?"

"Shut up, Sam! Don't yell at her!" Josh turned

quickly to Corina, his heart racing in his chest. He could see the fear and confusion in her eyes and knew she could see the same emotions in his own gaze. “Look, something is going down so we need to stick together. The adults aren’t going to understand until it is too late.”

“Yeah, just like in the movies,” Troy agreed.

“Parents never listen in the movies,” Josh grimly continued. “And they’re not going to listen in real life.”

“You don’t know that,” Corina said shortly. “You’re not making sense! None of this is making sense!”

Another bus pulled out as cars honked and a father ran along the side of it shouting for the bus driver to stop. Short, hard pops, which sounded like fireworks, began to go off somewhere nearby.

“That’s gunfire,” Josh exclaimed.

“Get to the bus! Get to the bus!” Mrs. Adkins rushed over and grabbed Sam’s hand. “Hurry up, boys! Stop dawdling!”

“C’mon,” Josh ordered his small group of Zombie

Hunters and they marched toward the nearest bus. "We'll get to the community center then plan from there. We gotta get out of here before the zombies arrive."

Two sheriff cars roared past the school toward the highway, lights flashing and sirens howling. Across the street, the high school parking lot was emptying as cars drove over the curbs and lawn to pull onto the roadway.

"Josh! Josh!" his mother's voice cried out.

"Mom!"

Lynette rushed up to him, her face drained of color beneath her mussed hair. She hugged him, and he could feel her heart racing in her chest.

"Are you okay?"

"I'm fine! What is going on, Mom?"

"There is something going down on the highway. We all need to get to the community center. We'll be safe there."

"Rescue centers are never safe," Troy said sorrowfully. "It always goes wrong there."

"Yeah," his brother agreed.

"Well, that is where you boys need to go!" Lynette said shortly. "All of you need to get on that bus."

"Mom, I want to go with you!"

"Josh, I need you to get on that bus. I have to go get Drake at daycare. I'll meet you at the community center."

"Mom, is what they say true? Are those crazy people here?"

The expression on his mom's face was almost as terrifying as the screams and gunshots in the distance. She nodded, her lips pressed together. "Get on the bus, Josh. I want to know you're safe. I heard the National Guard is on its way to the community center." As she talked, his mom pulled him toward the next bus being loaded, his friends in their wake.

"Mom, I want to go with you!"

"No, Josh. I need you safe. Do you understand? I will get Drake and join you. Please, just go!" Lynette kissed his cheek, hugging him again. "I need to know you're safe."

“Mom, please let me go with you!” Josh held onto her as tight as he could, but she pried his arms from around her.

“I’ll see you soon! I love you! Get on the bus!” She darted back into the crowd, running toward the parking lot.

For once no one uttered a word about his mom being hot and Josh was grateful. Corina placed her hand on his shoulder, a reassuring gesture, and Josh appreciated it. They were getting closer to the bus as the line advanced and his heart beat fiercely in his chest with anticipation. Sweat trickled from his hairline, getting in his eyes. He could hear Sam wheezing behind him as Arturo told him to shut up. Troy and Roger were quiet, their expressions tense.

“Maybe we should go see if Dad is coming,” Roger said after a few seconds.

“He was on the phone. I think he was calling the army or something,” Troy answered. His face was etched with fear. “He said for us to get on the bus.”

“I think I want to go be with Dad,” Roger answered, his voice sounding higher in pitch than usual.

"We just need to get to the community center and our folks will meet us there," Josh assured them. He didn't want to tell them about Mr. Johnson probably being infected and that their father was in danger. He considered running back inside to warn the adults, but he already knew they weren't going to listen to him.

"The rescue centers aren't safe!" Roger exclaimed.

"Calm down, Rog!" Troy shouted at his brother.

"You calm down!"

"Dude, I'm chill!"

"I want dad!"

"Both of you chill out!" Josh ordered.

He was surprised when they both lapsed into silence. Sam chewed on his bottom lip, breathing through his nose, sounding like a beached whale. Corina kept tugging on her ponytails, obviously nervous. Josh wanted to comfort her, but didn't know how.

Another bus departed, the crowd thinning out.

Parents continued to arrive, desperate to find their children.

"Where is my girl?" a man shouted at Mrs. Adkins.

"She already left on the bus," she answered. "She's going to the community center."

"You have no right to remove my child from the school without my permission!" the man screamed into Mrs. Adkins' face.

Josh finally reached the bus and climbed onto the first step. He glanced nervously at the man confronting Mrs. Adkins. He didn't look infected, just angry.

"Hurry up, son," the driver said, motioning down the aisle.

"We need to evacuate the school! We had no choice!" Mrs. Adkins answered heatedly. "We're doing our-"

There was a loud slap of skin against skin, then sharp cry as the students gasped.

"He hit her!" Corina cried out. "He hit her!" She dropped out of line, rushing back to help Mrs.

Adkins.

"No, Corina," Josh shouted after her, trying to turn back.

"Keep moving! Keep moving!" the bus driver ordered, catching his arm and pushing him back up the steps. "Don't slow down the line!"

Josh reluctantly shuffled into the aisle; Roger and Troy close behind him. The seats were filling up quickly. Crushed together, some of the children sobbed while others looked too scared to do anything but stare out at the mayhem. Reaching the back of the bus, the three boys squeezed into one of the remaining seats. Looking out the window, Josh strained to see if he could spot his mom's car out in the parking lot. It was packed. The cars of teachers and parents maneuvered around each other as they were trying to leave.

"I think we should go check on Dad," Roger said in a soft voice to his brother.

"If Dad wants us, he'll come get us. Just like all the other parents," Troy answered shortly.

Arturo and Sam slid into the seat behind them. It

was obvious that Sam had decided to stay close to them. He chewed on his bottom lip while Arturo looked annoyed to be saddled with him.

Josh strained to see toward the front of the bus, hoping to see Corina. He wished she hadn't turned back to help Mrs. Adkins.

"If you can't find a seat, just stand up! Hold onto the back of the seats!" The bus driver was pushing kids down the aisle to cries of protest.

"You're gonna smash us to death!" Sam shouted.

"Shut up, freak!" Arturo snapped. He shoved his black hair out of his face as he leaned toward Josh. "Dude, we should have gone with your mom."

"She's getting Drake. She told us to get on the bus," Josh answered. His hand was trembling as he placed it on the back of the seat in front of him. He felt sick with fear and he looked out the window again, trying to spot his mom's car.

"Whoa, Mrs. Adkins got hit hard," Troy said in awe.

Their teacher stumbled onto the bus, holding her hand over one eye, blood trickling out of the corner of her mouth. The bus driver made some of the kids stand so she could sit down. Corina was nowhere to be seen. Josh's heart beat a little harder as fear gripped him. He returned his gaze to the parking lot, praying softly.

"Please, God...please, God...please, God..."

Finally, Josh caught sight of his mom's old blue Chevy in line to get out of the parking lot. He could barely make out her figure inside the car, the sun glinting off her hair. He wanted to crawl out the window and run to her. Fear had a brutal grip on him, and he just wanted to feel her arms around him.

The sound of a motorcycle cut through the noise as Brad roared up to the bus. "Corina! Corina!"

Screams erupted again outside, but this time, they sounded different. It was more than fear that tinged the shrieks. A bus roared past, nearly clipping Brad on his bike. Cars began to honk desperately.

"Oh, my God," Arturo exclaimed.

All the kids in the bus turned around at once.

A pack of bloody, mutilated people had come around the side of the school moving relentlessly toward the children and adults still loading onto the last school bus. All had faces smeared with blood. One of them appeared to be carrying a dismembered leg.

"Zombies!" a kid shouted, then everyone on the bus began crying or shrieking.

CHAPTER 9

Josh briefly saw Corina dart past the end of the bus before vanishing from view again. Nearby, a man climbed out of his truck and reached back into the cab to grab his hunting rifle. He began firing at the advancing figures. The bloody people jerked as the bullets tore through their flesh as they kept advancing.

"The head! The head!" Troy yelled at the guy. "Shoot 'em in the head!"

Other kids picked up the chant.

Another man and a woman also grabbed guns out of their cars and began to fire at the creatures. Covered in blood, the undead bodies jerked and stumbled as they tried to walk toward the buses. They looked exactly like the monsters in the movies.

It was a scene out of Josh's worst nightmares. It couldn't be real. He rubbed his eyes before looking out the back windows again.

The zombies were still there.

"Go! Go! Go!" Arturo shouted at the bus driver.

Josh turned to look toward his mother's car. The blue vehicle was still stuck in line to get out of the parking lot. Brad's motorcycle, with Corina clinging to him, swerved in and out of the buses and cars clogging the bus lane.

"Go! Go! Go!" some of the children began to chant, while the others shouted, "Shoot 'em in the head!"

Josh looked back to see another mangled figure fall to the ground before climbing back to its feet. The teachers, driver and coaches herded the remaining students onto the last bus. Parents grabbed up their children and ran for their cars.

“The head! The head!” Sam yelled. “Shoot ‘em in the head!”

A mud splattered truck roared through the group of staggering zombies, knocking them aside. It sped past the last of the buses and children, driving over the sidewalk as it tried to escape.

The driver of their bus continued to try to load the last of the students onto his vehicle. The children were already crammed into the narrow aisle and falling over onto those already seated.

“We need to go now!” Arturo shouted at the driver.

The first of the zombies reached out toward a father carrying his child to his car. It made a mad grab for him, looking almost comical as it missed and fell to the ground.

“Maybe they are *Night of the Living Dead* zombies,” Troy said, rubbing his chin thoughtfully.

“I want Dad!” Roger cried out suddenly. He began to get out of his seat. “I want Dad!”

“Dude, no! Calm down! We gotta get out of

here," Josh said quickly, trying to push Roger back into his seat.

"No, no! I want Dad! I want my dad!" Roger pushed against Troy as the other boy tried to hold him back.

"No, bro, no! We gotta stay on the bus!"

"I want my dad!" Roger shrieked, his face flushed red and his eyes streaming tears.

"He's losing it!" Sam exclaimed.

"Shut up!" Arturo punched Sam in the arm.

Josh tried to help Troy keep Roger from crawling over the back of the seat in front of them. As he struggled with the other boy, he saw fast movement outside the bus windows.

"Running zombies!" Josh gasped.

"Oh, man. That is totally the *Dawn of the Dead* remake!" Arturo wailed.

The new arrivals didn't have the horrible disfigurement of the first group of zombies. They did have blood on them, but their legs weren't broken or severely damaged, so they were fast.

Terrifyingly fast.

Josh's heart beat so hard in his chest it actually hurt. The edges of his vision blurred as he turned to look for his mom's car. It took a few seconds for him to find it near the edge of the parking lot. His mother was trying to edge between two parked cars and up onto the sidewalk. The world grew dimmer and slower as he saw running zombies pouring into the parking lot.

"Mom," he whispered.

"I want my dad!" Roger screamed just before he managed to vault himself over the back of the seat onto the kids seated before him.

Troy scrambled after him. "Roger!"

"Oh, man!" Sam exclaimed. "They got someone!"

There was a pack of the zombies gathering around someone on the ground.

"This isn't real," Arturo said, clenching his eyes shut. "This isn't real!"

Josh turned to look toward his mom's car again. The things were swarming it, beating on the windows, growling at her.

"Mom," Josh murmured, his throat constricting

with fear.

A massive truck slammed into one of the parked cars blocking his Mom's car, the squeal of tires and warping metal filling the air. The truck kept ramming the car until it finally gave way and was shoved up onto the sidewalk. The truck pushed through as the zombies beat on the sides of it. To Josh's relief, his mom's car followed. He lost sight of her car as she managed to get onto the main road behind the treeline.

Finally, their bus began to move as the running creatures drew near. Josh could see the zombies smashing their hands and even their heads, against the glass of the cars still trying to escape the pandemonium in the parking lot and bus lane. All around him, other students tried to close the windows, though there was little chance of the zombies managing to reach that high. Roger and Troy struggled with each other, falling into the other kids, who shoved them away.

"Children, calm down! We're getting away!" Mrs. Adkins shouted from the front of the bus. She stood behind the driver's seat, holding onto the pole. Her face was swollen, but she managed to still get the attention of the kids.

The driver swore as he tried to get past a car blocking his way. There was no sign of the driver. Screams, growls, and moans assaulted Josh's ears along with the gunning of engines and the sharp squeal of brakes. He looked down into the bus lane to see a father and son fighting off two of the zombies. The father was swinging his now empty rifle at the creatures as his child used his backpack like a shield. The bus managed to get past the stalled car and Josh lost sight of the two as the bus rolled on. Smoke was rising from a car that had crashed into another. Flames licked along the edges of the hood. The zombies gathered around both cars, reaching in to bite and tear at the people inside.

"Thisisn'trealthisisn'trealthisisn'treal..." Arturo chanted, his eyes still closed as he rocked in his seat.

Sam watched with his mouth hanging open, a tiny bit of drool collecting in each corner.

"Mr. Inmon is coming! So is Mr. Johnson!" a little girl called out from the other side of the bus.

"Dad!" Roger stopped fighting with his brother and scrambled over a few older boys to look out the window.

Josh stood up on his seat, steadying himself with one hand on the window frame. This couldn't be good. He had seen the wounds on Mr. Johnson. Over the tops of the heads of the others on the bus, he could see Mr. Inmon running toward the bus, yelling for the driver to open the doors. Behind him, Mr. Johnson ran in pursuit, blood pouring out of his mouth.

"Don't let Mr. Johnson in! Don't let him in!" Josh shouted.

"You need to stop for my dad!" Roger tried to push his way through the crowded aisle, but his brother managed to hold onto his hoodie and keep him back.

Mr. Inmon reached out frantically toward the bus as he ran. Blood stained his shirt.

Josh felt his stomach knot with fear. "I don't

think we should let Mr. Inmon in! He might be infected!"

"I want my dad! Let him on the bus!" Roger shouted.

"No, you can't! He's infected!"

"You shut up, Josh! You shut up!"

The bus was slowing down as it maneuvered down the cluttered bus lane. Josh's heart beat loudly in his ears. He could see some zombies running alongside the bus out of the corner of his eye.

"Don't stop!" Josh yelled again, but his voice was drowned out by the others.

Mr. Inmon's skinny frame picked up speed as he drew closer to the bus. Josh saw Mrs. Adkins pulling the lever that opened the doors. Returning his gaze to Mr. Inmon, Josh drew in a sharp breath that hurt all the way down to his ribs.

He saw a bite on Mr. Inmon's neck.

Mr. Johnson continued his chase, his hands slashing out to grab Mr. Inmon. The school nurse also followed, her neck a mass of ruined flesh.

"...this isn't real..." Arturo continued to chant.

Mrs. Adkins stumbled backward as Mr. Inmon leaped onto the bus. He fell across the steps and out of view as the passengers all screamed for Mrs. Adkins to shut the door.

"Dad! Dad! Dad!" Roger shouted, fighting to get away from Troy.

The bus accelerated as Mr. Johnson leaped for the doorway. Josh started to scream along with the other students for Mrs. Adkins to shut the door, but instead she bent down to help Mr. Inmon. Mr. Johnson's bloodied hands grabbed the edge of the doorway and his huge frame filled the doorway. Mrs. Adkins cried out as he lashed out, grabbing her by her hair.

The bus driver swore loudly, grabbing the lever to shut the door. With a loud growl, Mr. Johnson yanked Mrs. Adkins into his arms before they both tumbled out of the bus.

The students fell into a terrified silence as the teacher and principal disappeared from view. Tears flowing down his cheeks, Josh turned to watch the school nurse join Mr. Johnson as he tore at Mrs. Adkins. Behind the bus, the other ravaged zombies followed. Some ran, but most shambled.

Hardly able to catch his breath, Josh looked back toward the front of the bus.

"Get up! Get up!" the bus driver shouted at Mr. Inmon. "I have to shut the door!"

The bus rumbled out onto the main road. The students looked back toward the school in shock. The zombies feasted on their victims as cars burned in the parking lot. A few people ran on foot from the school toward the parking lot with zombies following close behind. A huge fireball burst out of one of the burning cars, tossing it over onto another car. Smoke billowed into the blue sky as the last bus rode out of the school grounds behind them.

"Dad! Dad!" Roger cried out.

"Josh, my dad!" Troy reached out to grip Josh's wrist, looking up at him. "My dad...did you see?"

"Yeah," Josh answered. Sweat was pouring into his eyes, making it hard to see. His hands shook as he tried to brace himself as he stood on his seat.

"Yeah, I saw."

"Get up! I gotta close the doors," the driver again shouted at Mr. Inmon. His face was slick with sweat and as he spoke spittle flew from his thin lips. "Get up!"

"In the movies, this is always a bad moment," Josh said to Troy.

Troy's dark skin had taken on a gray appearance as he swallowed hard. "I know. My dad, Josh...my dad...We gotta get outta here."

"I want my dad!" Roger kept trying to break free from his brother.

The bus turned down a side road where old trailers and dilapidated houses listed in tall grasses as the driver tried to get away from the cars beginning to clog the street.

Tears ran down Troy's face as he began to push other kids aside, trying to get to the back door. He dragged Roger behind him. Josh leaned over and smacked Arturo in the head and his friend's eyes flew open.

"We need to get out here! Mr. Inmon was

bitten!"

"That's bad, right? That's bad?" Sam looked terrified.

A terrifying shriek from the front of the bus sent icy chills over Josh's scalp and down his spine. He looked over his shoulder to see Mr. Inmon rise up and grab the driver's head between his hands. With another awful shriek, Mr. Inmon whipped his head forward and drove his teeth into the man's face.

CHAPTER 10

The steering wheel spun in the driver's hands as he flailed about in his seat trying to fight off his attacker. The bus veered off the road, bouncing over the uneven terrain and through a fence. Josh fell into the seat in front of him as the bus crashed through bushes and the low hanging branches of trees bordering the property of a dilapidated, burned out trailer listing in tall grass. It slammed into the side of a mobile home, knocking it completely off its cement block foundation. Finally, the bus came to a brutal stop as it buried itself into the twisted metal and fiberglass.

"Get Josh! Get him!" Troy shouted at his brother, scrabbling to get a grip on Josh.

Elbows and hands dug into him as the young people Josh had fallen into tried to push him off them. The screams, shouts, and cries of the terrified students filled the bus and drowned out the sounds of flesh tearing as Mr. Inmon devoured the driver's face.

Arturo and Troy managed to get a good grip on Josh's jeans and yanked him over the back of the seat.

Josh immediately twisted around, pulling his backpack straps tighter. "We need to get out of here now!"

"I want my dad," Roger sobbed softly, his gaze unfocused as he stared toward the front of the bus.

The remains of the mobile home enshrouded the driver's seat and first few rows in darkness.

"We can't save dad!" Troy shouted at his brother. "We gotta save ourselves!"

An older boy pushed aside some of the younger kids crowded around the emergency door to try to open it while others struggled to get their windows down. The students in the front of the bus scrambled to the back of the bus, climbing over seats and other passengers. The crush of bodies at the rear of the bus was almost unbearable as Josh joined Troy, Roger, Arturo and Sam in their cramped seat. Screams filled the cramped space.

"Open the door!"

"I'm trying," the older boy shouted in reply. "It's jammed!"

Josh dared to look toward the front of the bus. It was so dark he could barely make out the form of Mr. Inmon leaning over the bus driver, tearing at him like a lion eating a gazelle in a documentary.

Another boy grabbed the lever and helped pull. It gave way with a moan and the door swung open. The first boy leaped down, then reached up to help the others down.

"Hurry! Hurry!" was the chant of the students trapped inside the bus as they surged forward.

Josh and the other boys pushed as hard as they could to get out of their seat and into the aisle, but the onslaught from the front was steady. Smaller children cried out in agony as they were smashed into seats.

“Stop pushing! Stop pushing!” someone shouted.

The two bigger boys quickly helped the children down, but the pushing from the students trapped in the front of the bus was relentless.

A blood curdling scream ripped through the cries of the other children. It was the most terrifying sound Josh had ever heard. Glancing over his shoulder to see what was happening, he only saw the terrified faces of his classmates as the pressure from the front grew unbearable. He couldn’t breathe, he couldn’t move and his feet were twisted around someone else’s.

“They got Mary! They got her! They got her!” a voice rose in a terrified screech from the front.

All sense of order was lost. Josh felt himself being shoved toward the back door, his feet no longer under him. He was held upright by the bodies of the other terrified children.

Troy and Roger hit the doorway, both of them managing to jump at the last moment. Josh couldn't catch himself fast enough and tumbled out. He landed in a soft patch of earth and grass, his backpack smacking him in the back of the head. Another kid landed near him, crying out as he landed on his knees.

Crawling away as fast as he could, Josh's fingers sank into the soil. Terror pulled at his rational mind, spurring him to panic, but he fought against it. He had to keep his wits about him. Someone grabbed his arm and dragged him to his feet.

"Thanks, man," Josh gasped, seeing it was Arturo.

Arturo wasn't looking at him though. His gaze was on the bus.

Josh turned to see that several windows toward the midsection of the bus were covered in thick red blood and darker, meatier globs.

"Dude, they're eating us," Arturo whispered.

The first big group of kids to evacuate the bus ran

down the road, their footfalls pounding against the asphalt. The two older boys remained to help the last of the kids out of the bus.

"You need to close the door as soon as they're out," Josh told the boys. "You need to keep those things trapped in there!"

A little girl, her brown curls in disarray around her face, reached down for help. Her pink tunic top was covered in pretty flowers and splashes of fresh blood. Her white leggings and pink shoes were also stained with blood. One of the boys grabbed her and dragged her down to the ground. Taking a deep breath, the little girl let out a whimper.

A group of boys were next, casting terrified looks over their shoulder. They, too, had blood splatter on them.

"Josh, let's go," Arturo said, grabbing his arm. "C'mon!"

The little girl stumbled over to a battered lawn chair and sat down, tears streaming down her face. She was shivering and pale.

"We need to help her," Josh decided, hurrying

over to the girl. He saw Troy and Sam dragging Roger away toward the street. Roger fought them, crying out for his father.

"We're the last ones," a girl, an eighth grader that was a friend of Corina's, said as she reached down to the boys. "They got four of us kids. Hurry!"

The two helpers grabbed hold of her arms and started to help her down. Behind her, another boy grabbed hold of the doorjamb, ready to leap out.

"C'mon," Josh said to the little girl, gripping her hand. "We need to go."

"They ate Mary," the little girl answered him, fumbling with her pocket. She was wheezing loudly, her tiny fingers sweaty in his hand.

"I know. But c'mon."

Josh pulled her to her feet as she drew an inhaler from her pocket. She couldn't be older than six. Dragging her behind him, he ran past the end of the bus. His brain felt mushy and he was having trouble moving. It was like being in a bad dream where your feet were like concrete slabs and you could barely run.

Just as the older female student landed on the ground, the boy behind her gasped in pain. Two sets of small hands grabbed his sides and tugged him backwards. He fell into the darkness of the bus.

"Shut the door!" Josh shouted.

"My brother!" Corina's friend screamed.

One of the boys grabbed the door and tried to slam it shut, but it bounced off the bloodied, torn hands thrusting out toward them. Josh continued to run, trying to watch where he was going while still keeping an eye on the bus. The little girl stumbled after him as she tried to run while taking a quick hit on her inhaler at the same time.

"Close it!" one of the older boys cried out. "Hurry!"

The shouts behind him continued as the two boys struggled to shut the door and someone inside, either a zombie or wounded person, fought to push it open. Finally, the door latched, blood seeping out beneath the nearly severed fingers poking out from beneath the edge of it. The older kids ran past Josh and the little girl, shouting at each other to hurry.

"Pick up the pace, shorty!" one of the boys huffed as he passed Josh.

Up ahead, the children ran to the main road, making far too much noise in Josh's opinion. They were going to attract attention with all the screaming and yelling they were doing. His own friends were toward the back of the pack, Sam falling further behind every second.

"Stop, Roger! Stop, Troy! Arturo! We're going the wrong way!" Josh cried out. "Come back!"

Josh stopped, trying to calm his panicked nerves. He held tightly to the little girl's hand. She didn't fight with him, staring blankly ahead. Taking deep breaths, Josh tried to organize his thoughts.

The neighborhood around him was silent. It was a work day and most of the people in this poor section of town were at their jobs. Also, a lot of the houses were derelict. The world around them was nearly silent except for the pounding on the back door of the bus, the ticking of the bus engine cooling off, and the birds in the trees. In the far distance, he could hear horns honking and the sound of guns firing.

Above the town, the sky was growing dark with thick rain clouds. Without the sun, the day felt colder and he shivered in his hoodie. His friends argued as the other students ran toward the main street, leaving them far behind. Roger pulled at his hair as Troy and Arturo yelled at each other. Sam was the first to turn back. He trudged toward Josh, his big body heaving with exertion. Finally, the three members of the Zombie Hunter Club turned back, running as fast as they could.

Josh kept an eye on the bus as his friends sprinted toward him. He could feel the muscles in his back tensing as another shiver of fear flowed over him. Looking around at the neighborhood, he made his plan.

"Dude, what are we doing? Everyone ran that way! And zombies are in that bus!" Troy said, pointing at the bus and the figures moving inside of it.

"I know. But they're running toward the main road. The zombies that came off the highway are over there! They're not thinking straight. We need to take these back roads to the community center. Everyone is at work right now. People aren't at home. Less zombies this way." Josh pointed down the long strip of road leading to a slow curve lined on both sides with juniper trees and old, battered homes.

"I think we should stick with the older kids," Arturo answered. "They're stronger than us and maybe the can get a car for us."

"For a busload of kids?" Josh looked at him incredulously.

"Whatever we're gonna do, we gotta do it soon. Those zombies can see us and they want to eat us. So let's go," Troy said firmly.

"I want dad," Roger mumbled, wiping his eyes.

"Your dad wants you for dinner," Sam yelled at him. "Shut up!

Arturo slugged Sam in the stomach. "No, you shut up!"

"Ow! Josh, he hit me!"

"Let's get out of here," Josh ordered. "You two

cut it out! Stop fighting. Roger, we can't save your dad."

"Who's the girl, Josh?" Troy asked, noticing the wheezing child for the first time.

"Yessica," the girl answered. She sniffled loudly.

"We need to take care of her," Josh answered. "She's got no one else."

Troy glanced over his shoulder at the kids disappearing around the corner. A few were straggling behind, out of breath. "Okay, fine. Let's move."

"Are you sure we shouldn't go with the older kids?" Arturo also looked back toward the main road.

Josh was about to answer when the first running zombie made its appearance. It sprinted across the mouth of the road after the last of the students.

Without a word, the Zombie Hunters began to run in the opposite direction. Josh held to Yessica's hand, feeling her slick fingers gripping his tightly. Troy ran a little ahead of them, Roger keeping pace with Josh. Arturo and Sam took up the rear, Sam breathing heavily. Josh was worried about him and Yessica falling behind. He was determined not to lose anyone.

Troy veered off the road into a yard. He snatched up an aluminum baseball bat discarded near some outdoor toys. Arturo and Sam followed, each looking around for a weapon. Scanning the yard, Josh felt his heart beating faster. He needed a weapon and soon. Seeing a stick lying in a pile of branches piled up near the road for the city to pick up, he pulled Yessica behind him. The stick was still green in the center and when he whacked it against another branch, it made a satisfying thwacking sound.

"I want my dad," Roger wailed as he waited for his brother.

"Snap out of it, Rog!" Troy smacked the mailbox with the bat on the way over to his brother. "Dad is dead and now he wants to eat us."

Roger sobbed harder, his whole body shaking. "Don't say that!"

"Well, it's true." Sam swung a battered tennis

racket back and forth in front of him. “He wants to eat us.”

“No,” Roger answered. “You take that back!”

“But it’s true!” Sam protested. “He wants to eat us!”

Josh looked back toward the bus imbedded in the side of the trailer. They were only a half block away from it. Looking toward the end of the road, he saw more of the fast zombies running after the students who had been foolish enough to head down the main road. Luckily, none of the monsters looked their way.

“We need to go now.” Josh’s voice was firm. It drew everyone’s attention to him. “Now. No more fighting. Do you want to end up eaten like those kids on the bus? Or at the school? I don’t. So let’s go!”

Without looking back to see if they were following, Josh began to run toward the long curve in the road ahead. He knew it would skirt around the edge of town before meeting up with some of the neighborhood roads south of town.

Yessica ran beside him, clutching her inhaler. She still looked pale and frightened. He wondered if she was in shock. He heard the footfalls of his friends behind him and their lowered voices as they kept arguing. His brain felt clearer now. He drank in deep breaths of cool spring air, trying to get a plan formed in his mind.

"Josh! Josh!" Sam's voice cried out.

"Dangit, Sam! Keep it down. They'll hear us," Josh answered, glancing back toward Sam.

"He's coming," was all Sam managed to call out as he tried to pick up his pace, breathing even harder.

"Who's coming?" Troy asked, running with his hand firmly on his brother's shoulder, guiding him forward.

Josh's eyes widened as he caught sight of the figure not too far behind them. "Your dad," he answered.

CHAPTER 11

Josh felt his heart skip a beat and his legs felt like rubber. Fear rose up, choking him and making it hard to speak.

The zombie that was once Roger and Troys' father was covered in blood and moving rapidly toward them. His body jerked as his feet skittered across the asphalt. It was if he had forgotten how to move like a human. The zombie continued his soundless rush toward them. Since his throat was ripped out, zombie Mr. Inmon's mouth was open in a silent scream, blood drizzling down his front.

"Josh!" Sam exclaimed. "What are we going to do?"

Finally, Josh answered in a low voice, "Keep running!"

"Dad! Dad!" Roger wailed as Troy shoved him down the road. "My dad is hurt!"

"He's not hurt, Rog!" Troy yanked on his arm, trying to get him to run.

The boys struggled with each other, sweat pouring down their faces despite the chill in the air.

Overhead, the sky rumbled, briefly distracting Josh. Drawing a deep breath, he tried to focus the flurry of thoughts whirling around in his mind. Arturo barreled past Josh and Yessica, pumping his arms and legs as hard as he could. Fear painted his features into a dull color, his eyes stark in his terrified expression. Josh tried to reach out to him, but Arturo kept running, his breath ragged.

Lumbering toward them, sweat making his red face slick and shiny, Sam grunted and groaned with determination. His huge stomach swayed back and forth as he pushed himself harder than Josh had ever seen before. Not even in gym class. Sam had always resisted doing any physical activity until now. Of course, he had never had zombies running after him before.

"Take Yessica with you," Josh ordered Sam, holding out her hand out to him. "I'm going to get the zombie."

Sam nodded, hardly able to breathe, and grabbed the little girl's hand, yanking her after his lumbering body. Yessica let out a small yelp, startled, clearly not really comprehending what was going on. Her tiny body looked fragile next to Sam's as they ran.

"What are you gonna do, Josh?" Troy called out, still trying to get his brother under control. The tiny droplets of sweat in his hair made his afro sparkle.

Josh watched the bloody man rushing toward him while he pulled his backpack off his shoulders. "I'm gonna be a Zombie Hunter and stop him." His heart was pounding so hard against his ribs that it hurt.

"No!" Roger whirled around, knocking Troy

aside. “Josh, leave my dad alone!”

Arturo doubled back and slammed into Roger, tackling him to the ground before the distraught boy could run toward his zombiefied father. The three boys wrestled on the ground, Arturo and Troy trying to get Roger under control. With grim determination, Sam ran past the ruckus, pulling the little girl along with him.

Swinging his heavy pack down to his side, Josh narrowed his eyes on the creature running toward him. Mr. Inmon’s face was unrecognizable. Bloody teeth gnashing, hands slashing out in front of him, Roger and Troy’s father was more terrifying than Josh could have ever imagined. Josh coughed; his breath still caught in his throat, and tried to keep his balance as the world seemed to sway around him. This was it. He was going to kill a zombie. He was going to kill the father of his friends. The coppery smell of blood filled his nostrils and he felt faint, like he was going to throw up.

“You have to do this,” he grimly told himself.

“Don’t hurt my dad!”

Troy and Arturo fought with Roger, trying to get him to his feet and away. Roger, who was not about to give in to them, scrabbled along the road toward Josh.

"Run, Roger! It's not your dad anymore," Josh ordered.

"Leave my dad alone!"

Mr. Inmon was almost to them, his legs jerking oddly as he ran. There was no more time. Either he had to run away and hope his three friends followed or make his stand. He felt he had no choice. As terrifying as this moment was, it was what he had been preparing for all along.

"Please work," Josh prayed. "Please work."

"Don't hurt my Dad!"

Josh swung his backpack as hard as he could, aiming for the zombie's lower legs. For a brief, awful second, he was sure he was going to fail as the backpack arced through the air. Then it slammed into Mr. Inmon's ankles. The zombie tripped, flailing about as he kept trying to reach his next meal, his feet becoming tangled in the straps.

Hands flung out to grab Josh, zombie Mr. Inmon fell. Unlike a living human being, he didn't even try to catch himself. His dead gaze was fastened firmly on Josh as he slammed headfirst into the asphalt. There was a loud crack as his skull impacted with the ground. Thick, dark blood began to ooze out from around his head as the zombie that used to be Mr. Inmon lay motionless.

Josh let out an explosive breath, his chest heaving. He hadn't even realized he had been holding it. He stumbled back a few feet, trying to calm his harshly beating heart.

"Did you kill it?" Arturo called out in awe.

Josh could see that the side of Mr. Inmon's head was bashed in. "Yeah. Yeah, I think I did."

"No!" Roger screamed. "No!" He wrenched free of the other two boys, scrambled to his feet, and ran toward his dad.

"No, Rog!" Josh grabbed for him, but Roger evaded him.

Falling to his knees, Roger took hold of his father's shoulder and began to shake him. "Dad, wake up! Dad, wake up!"

Fearfully, Josh picked up the tree branch he had chosen as a weapon and moved closer to the fallen zombie. "Roger, get away from him. We can't be sure he's really dead."

"Dad, please wake up. Please, wake up," Roger sobbed. Tears streamed down his face.

His footsteps sounding heavy on the ground, Troy bounded over to them, the baseball bat held over his head. "Let's go. Let's go! If he got out, the others might, too!"

"I think his brain is leaking out on the ground," Arturo said in awe, daring to join them.

Josh moved around the zombie's body and pulled his backpack from Mr. Inmon's ankles. The zombie remained unmoving. Josh couldn't bear to see the emptiness in his eyes or how his torn, bloody mouth hung open, his tongue touching the dirty road.

"Dad, please," Rog cried, shaking his father harder.

"Let's go!" Troy grabbed his brother's arm. "Now! We need to get to Mom, Rog!"

Roger blinked slowly, and then looked up at his brother. "Mom?"

"Yeah, Rog. Let's go get Mom. Now!"

With Arturo and Troy's help, Roger got to his feet. His expression was like that of someone slowly waking up, but not fully understanding their surroundings yet.

Josh looked up to see that Sam and Yessica were near the curve in the road. Their pace was slow, but at least they were safely away. Glancing back toward the bus, he could see the figures inside trying to find their way out. At the mouth of the road, there were figures shambling, moving in the direction in which the other students had fled.

"We need to go. Roger, get it together. Now." Josh wasn't sure if he could fight off any more zombies. He already felt sick to his stomach about Mr. Inmon. He knew he had been lucky. His plan had been desperate and he hadn't expected Mr. Inmon to crack his skull open. He had thought he would have to smash it in with his stick.

"I want Mom," Roger said in a soft, strange voice.

"Okay, then let's go find her," Troy said, taking hold of Roger's arm and pushing him after Sam and Yessica.

Together, the brothers began to run up the road.

"Finally," Arturo grunted, following.

Josh tugged on his backpack and clutched his stick in his hand tightly. Out of the remains of the mobile home, a small figure dragged itself into view. It was so badly mangled, Josh wasn't sure if it was a boy or a girl. It was too messed up to move very quickly and it struggled to move out of the wreckage.

"I hate zombies," Josh whispered, turned and ran up the road.

CHAPTER 12

Once past the curve in the winding road with the crashed school bus out of view, the children finally stopped running, dropping down to a quick walking pace. On this back road, the houses were few and far between and set back from the road. Most of the structures were old trailers. A few dogs barked at them, the sharp sound splitting the air.

In the distance, Josh could hear the sound of thunder, the pops of gunfire, and what sounded like sirens, or maybe screams. The oak and cedar trees lining the road rustled in the cool wind that rushed before the coming storm. The birds were eerily silent. A grackle let out a questioning squawk, but no other birds answered.

Arturo took the lead, walking briskly, a metal rod from an old lawn chair clutched in one hand. Troy and Roger were right behind him. Roger was crying, his head down, his hands in tight fists at his side. With his hand resting firmly on his brother's shoulder, Troy walked with his head up, looking around, alert and ready. Sam and Yessica followed. She took another hit on her inhaler and offered it to Sam, who took it gratefully. He was dragging his feet, exhaustion etched in his chubby face. Josh took up the rear, holding his tree branch, watching the road behind them.

None of the other kids had seen the mangled child zombie emerge from the wreckage. Josh was certain it was too messed up to catch up with them and be any threat. But if it had gotten out, maybe the others would follow. His ears strained for the telltale sound of feet slapping against the road.

Slowly, the overgrown brush and trees started to give way to lawns that showed signs of being mowed once and awhile, and long driveways leading to houses in better condition.

Josh saw an old woman out on her porch, sitting in an old metal chair, watching the road.

"Don't you dare come mess with my garden!" she shouted at them, waving her cane angrily.

"There's zombies!" Arturo yelled back.

"Don't come causing trouble! I'll call the police!" the old woman screeched.

"Shut up, man. The zombies will hear you," Troy chided him.

"Maybe we should try and warn her," Sam said, looking worried.

"Don't you watch the movies? She's not going to pay attention, we'll waste time warning her, then the zombies will come and eat some of us!" Arturo shoved Sam angrily.

Yessica let out a soft sob, clutching her inhaler even tighter in her hand.

"Just keep moving," Josh said, his voice tired.

He just wanted to lie down and take a nap. "Just keep moving."

Up ahead was the first intersection they had seen in nearly two miles. It was a sign they had reached the main area of the town. A few cars rushed across the intersection a few blocks down.

"We're getting closer," Sam said with relief.

"Yeah, we can see that stupid," Arturo grumbled.

"Give him a break, okay?" Troy snapped.

"I want Mom."

"I know, Rog. We're going to her now." Troy shook his head at Arturo.

"What?"

"Give the fat kid a break, okay?"

"I'm not that fat," Sam protested.

"Yes, you are," Arturo corrected him.

"Yeah, you are," Yessica agreed. "Like a ball."

Sam started to yank his hand away from her, but saw she wasn't judging him, just stating the truth.

"Leave him alone." Josh moved up to Arturo's side. "We need to work together so we don't end up dead."

"Yeah," Troy agreed.

"I want Mom," Roger said again.

Yessica sniffled as she began to cry. "I want mine, too."

"We're going to go to the community center and they will be there. Okay?" Josh looked back down the road again. He felt a cold chill rush down his spine as he saw a very small figure rounding the bend. The zombie was following them.

"How close are we?" Arturo asked.

"About six blocks. Three down. Three over."

"Josh, I'm so tired. Can we knock on a door and get some grownup to drive us?" Sam wiped his very red face with his thick fingers.

"I don't think we can risk the time to do that," Josh answered. "We got a zombie following us."

The kids all stopped to look back. Arturo slammed the metal rod in his hand against the road as Troy sighed. Yessica sobbed a little louder as Sam let out a soft hiss.

"It's Mary," Yessica wailed.

"It's far away. It's not gonna catch up unless we

stand here like idiots." Josh motioned them forward and the children trudged on.

Josh glanced into a few windows as they walked. Mostly the houses seemed empty, but he saw a few old people sitting in front of their TV sets. At one house a man was busy boarding up his windows. He saw the children, but pretended he hadn't. He was too consumed with saving himself to bother himself with them. A van tore through an intersection ahead of them.

Glancing back, Josh saw that the little girl zombie had vanished off the road. He thought of the mean old woman and felt a pang of guilt rip through him.

The loud buzzing, then first few notes of Chopin made all the children jump. Josh looked around in terror before realizing the vibration was coming from his backpack. It was his emergency cellphone. He had forgotten all about it. He was forbidden from using it except for absolute emergencies. Tearing off his backpack, he fumbled with the zipper of the pocket. He kept walking, glancing back toward where the child zombie had been just a few minutes before. Finally, he felt the small phone slide into his hand and flipped it open.

"Hello?"

"Josh, Josh!" It was his mother. Her voice was ragged and frantic.

"Yeah, Mom! It's me! It's me!"

"Are you at the community center?"

"No, Mom. The bus crashed. Me and my friends are trying to walk there now."

"Oh, God. Oh, God. Is there an adult with you?"

"No, Mom. They...uh...died."

"Oh, God." His mother lapsed into silence and he could hear Drake crying in the background.

"Mom?"

"Josh, I need you to come home. Can you do that?"

"Mom, I don't understand. You said to-"

"I know what I said. But I need you to come home. You need to come here right away."

"Can you come get me?"

"No, no, I can't. The car...I need you to come now. Okay? I want you to be very careful, avoid all the main streets, don't go near the daycare, and come straight here. Use the alleyways if you can."

Josh felt like he couldn't breathe anymore.

"Josh?"

"Okay, Mom."

"Send your friends to the community center and come home."

"Okay."

"If you see an adult, flag them down and see if they can bring you here, okay?"

"Yeah."

"Hurry, Josh," his mother said, then hung up.

Josh flipped the phone shut and looked up to see his friends staring at him.

"You had a phone the whole time?" Troy looked annoyed.

"Here," Josh answered, shoving it at him. "Call your Mom. I gotta go. My mom says I need to head home. You guys go to the community center. If you guys find an adult, send them to get me and my Mom and brother."

"Josh, don't leave us!" Sam cried out.

"You guys get to the community center! I'll see you later! Stay off the main roads, don't go near the daycare, stick to the alleys if you can. Go!"

Josh broke into a run away from them, cutting across a lawn to reach an alley that he knew would lead him to the street that would turn onto the one leading to his house. He could hear his friends protesting, but he couldn't wait for them. He knew something was terribly wrong and his stomach was clenching into a tight ball inside of him.

Running across an open street, lined with nicer homes with manicured lawns, Josh felt his chest burning as he struggled to breathe. Clothes, luggage, and toys were strewn across the grass, the driveways empty of cars. It looked like people had already fled this area. He didn't even hear dogs barking. Making a jagged run across several lawns, he scooted along the side of a house toward the alley.

Somewhere nearby, he heard a low moan that sent prickles of fear through him. Clutching his branch tighter, he leaped over some low bushes and into the alley. Running along the gravel passageway, he tried to keep his ears tuned to the sound of zombies.

Screams and shouts erupted nearby as an engine roared. There were a few short pops of a firearm, and then a station wagon sped past the mouth of the alley. It was full of people screaming.

"That's bad," he whispered, stopping in his tracks.

The road was a risk. Looking into the yard to his left, he saw it was clear. Crouching down, he ran alongside a hedge lining one side of the yard, moving toward the front of the house so he could see if the street was clear. He was closing in on his own home. It was only a block away.

The intersection was filled with wreckage. Five cars were crushed together, two of them on fire. Zombies were trapped inside of one of them. It wasn't too hard to imagine that someone had been injured and being rushed to the hospital when they had turned. Three dead zombies lay strewn along the side of the crash, bullet holes torn through their limbs and heads.

To Josh's horror, he realized one of the smoldering cars was his mother's blue Chevy. As he stared through the leaves of the bush he was hiding behind, he heard the low moans of zombies. Turning, he saw several moving down the road toward the crash. They had yet to see him. He burrowed into the bush, hoping they would pass him.

Shivering with fear, he held tightly to his branch as he heard the zombies dragging their feet past his hiding place. They moaned with hungry anticipation and he could feel his bowels churning. The last thing he wanted to do was crap himself. He clenched his body into a tight knot and prayed.

Finally, the moans drew away from him and he dared to look out toward the crash. The zombies were pawing at one of the cars, and Josh wondered if someone was trapped inside.

Looking around, he didn't see any more of the shambling creatures. It would be a risk, but he was sure he could make it across the street and into the yard of the house without being seen.

Taking a quick, hard breath, Josh shot out of the bush and raced across the street. He didn't even look toward the zombies. Instead he kept his eyes fastened on the fence lining the yard he was aiming to reach. He hit the grass and tore through the garden toward the back of the house.

If he could sprint through the yard just behind this house, he would exit onto the street where he lived. His house would be just a few houses down.

It wasn't a screech or a moan that let him know he was being pursued. It was the stomp of feet on the cement patio he had just sprinted across. He dared to look behind him and his heart jumped. It was a man, his face and neck torn, his shirt in shreds. The zombie clawed at the air as he rushed toward Josh. It was obvious he was one of the fast ones, one of the victims of the zombie plague that was not so torn up that he'd be slow and shambling.

Josh didn't even scream, but pushed his legs that much harder. He wove in between a playset and bright pink playhouse and leaped over a wagon, hoping the zombie would trip. He heard the crash of it running into the wagon, but from the sound of its footsteps behind him, it had quickly regained its balance.

Darting across the alley, Josh blinked hard, trying to get the sweat out of his eyes. It was hard to see as he ducked into the shade of huge pecan trees. He almost tripped over a sprinkler, but managed to avoid it.

Rushing through the shadows pooling alongside of the house he knew belonged to a nice elderly couple that gave his mother cookies and pies at holidays, he tried not to think of anything other than reaching his own home. If he could get to the door fast enough, he maybe could get inside before the zombie caught him.

Pouring all his energy into his run, Josh broke into the dappled sunlight and first drops of the coming rain. The sky was half overrun by dark clouds, but the sun still shone over this part of the town. Grunting, Josh sprinted toward the road, his home coming into view.

He was jolted to one side as the zombie briefly caught his backpack. Josh ducked and rolled, coming to his feet near a birdbath. He toppled it over as fast as he could. The zombie tripped over it, its hands barely missing him as it fell.

Not looking back, Josh ran as fast as he could toward his house. He could see that all the curtains were drawn. It looked as dead and silent as the rest of the houses on the street. His mother had to be there waiting for him. She had called him.

"Mom! Mom!" he shouted, risking that more zombies would come. "MOM!"

His legs were so tired he could feel his muscles cramping, but still he ran. The zombie snagged his backpack again, this time getting a firm grip. Josh brought his stick up as he pivoted, his feet tangling for a moment. He managed to ram it into the snapping jaws of the creature, point first, and shoved it hard. The zombie's head snapped back, its hands losing its grip on Josh's backpack. Josh yanked back from it, losing his balance and falling hard onto his bottom. Pain shot up his spine to spark in his eyes. The zombie howled then lunged toward him. Josh threw up his arm instinctively.

Three hard cracks of a pistol sounded.

"Stay away from him!"

More shots, then silence.

Josh lowered his arm to see the zombie lying dead near him. Jumping to his feet, he turned to see his mom standing in the doorway of their house.

The gun was still aimed at the zombie, her expression angry and fierce. Her blond hair spilled over her shoulders in golden curls. Josh thought she was the most beautiful thing he had ever seen.

"Get in the house, Josh," she said in a soft, yet commanding voice.

He obeyed her, walking swiftly toward the house. She kept the gun up, watching the road, her hand trembling.

It wasn't until she hugged him and scooted him in the doorway that he saw the strip of cloth wrapped around her arm and the dark, angry blob of red that could only mean one thing.

His mom had been bitten by a zombie.

CHAPTER 13

"Mom?" Josh whispered in a trembling voice as his mother slammed the door shut and twirled the locks.

Lynette rested her head against the door, taking in deep breaths. Drake, behind a child's gate erected between the kitchen and the dining room, was crying as he tried to climb over it.

Sweat slid down Josh's face, dripping off his chin as he slid off his backpack. He could feel his bottom lip quivering as he clenched his hands tightly at his side. He couldn't let himself fall apart. He had to be strong and take care of his family like he had promised his dad.

"Mom?"

"I'm so glad you made it. I was so scared you wouldn't." His mother's voice was soft, yet rough with emotion. Her eyes squeezed shut, tears rimming her eyelids and sparkling on her long lashes. Her lips trembled.

Josh threw his arms around her waist and clung to her. He felt her hand settle on his back as she quietly sobbed. It was her injured arm and he could smell the coppery scent of blood mixed with something putrid. His mother's body was very hot and he could feel her shivering.

"Mom?"

"I'm so glad you made it," she repeated in a soft, weary voice.

Drake managed to hoist himself over the top of the child gate and flopped onto the floor on the other side. He burst into loud, high-pitched cries.

"No, Drake," Lynette exclaimed. She wrenched

away from Josh and lurched across the living room. "Drake, stop crying. Stop! It will make the monsters come. Shhhhh."

Josh rushed around his obviously ailing mother and grabbed up Drake. His little brother felt heavy in his arms and to make matters worse, he flailed around, twisting his body to get away.

"Mama, Mama, Mama," Drake wailed.

"Drake, shhh, stop it!" Josh tried to cover his little brother's mouth, but Drake wrenched his tear and snot covered face away.

Lynette reached them and placed her hand against Drake's cheek, kissing his forehead. "Drake, be a good boy and stop crying. We don't want the monsters to come. No monsters, Drake," she whispered urgently against his skin.

Throwing his chubby arms around Lynette's neck, Drake clung to her, sobbing in a softer tone. "No monsters! They're bad! They hurt mama."

Lynette kissed him again as Josh looked warily at the windows. His mother had drawn the curtains, but there was nothing to keep the zombies out if they attacked. Looking back at his mother, he saw her gun tucked into the leather belt buckled around her slim waist. Slowly, he realized her long denim dress was stained with blood and torn along the side. Her heavily bandaged arm was still bleeding and blood dripped to the floor.

"Mom, did one of them bite you?" Josh could barely get the words out. His throat felt dry and painful as he spoke. He already knew the answer, but he wanted to believe he was wrong.

She nodded as she comforted Drake. Fresh tears slid down her cheeks as she held out her wounded arm. "I was trying to protect Drake."

It was hard to hear her over Drake's sobs. Josh again looked fearfully at the windows. His stupid little brother was going to get them eaten if he didn't shut up.

"Mom, let's get away from the windows, okay?"

Josh took hold of her good arm, guiding her through the archway to the hall near the stairs. The study was across from the stairway. It was a small room with only one window partially covered by a bookcase. The heavy velvet curtains were already closed. An old, battered green sofa sat against one wall and his grandfather's small desk was against another. His father's gun lockers were lined up against the wall, doors shut and padlocked.

His mother collapsed onto the sofa, clutching Drake with her one good arm. Her pale, sweat drenched skin looked sickly in the dim light seeping in around the edges of the curtains.

"Drake, go to your brother," Lynette ordered, her voice faint. She sounded tired and sad. Scooting the reluctant little boy off her lap, she gave him one last firm push toward Josh. "Mama needs to take a nap. You go with Josh."

Drake tried to resist, but Josh caught his wrist firmly, drawing him away.

"Mom," Josh said in a low voice, trying not to alert any nearby zombies to their whereabouts and also to keep his brother calm. "Mom, we need to go to the community center and get you a doctor."

Lynette shook her head, huge tears sliding down her cheeks. "I don't have that much time, Josh. I'll be...resting soon. I feel it inside...slowing everything down." She was trying to keep her voice even and not frighten Drake.

Distracted by a small iron statue of a cowboy on a horse, Drake wasn't paying much attention anyway. He was playing with the forbidden object, making it ride across the top of his grandfather's old wooden desk. His tears were drying on his face, his earlier tantrum forgotten.

"Mom, what happened?"

Lynette pulled a throw pillow up under her wounded arm. The wound was still seeping and the smell was foul.

"I got to his school and-"

"The monsters were there," Drake cut in. "They were bad. Like zombies." He went back to playing with the cowboy, pretending to fire the rifle the iron cast figure held.

"They had gotten into the building. Drake's teacher had the students barricaded in the room. When I got there, I saw her waving from the window. I could see from the tracks in the mud that other parents had driven up to the window, so I drove right up. There were only a few kids left and she begged me to get them all out. I guess the other parents had grabbed their kids and bailed. She told me she had been begging those other parents to get help so she could escape with the kids. There were zombies everywhere. Just then the door..."

"The bad monsters got in."

Lynette sighed, looking at her youngest with a sad expression. "They got in. Mrs. Hendricks grabbed Drake and pushed him through the window. I got him into the car and Mrs. Hendricks was trying to hand me another kid when...when...when..."

Tears streamed down Lynette's cheeks as the horror of the moment overwhelmed her. She wiped her tears away, smearing her makeup around her eyes. The blue wasn't as bright as before, as if a cloud was slowly moving over her irises.

"I got in the car and pulled out, but we got swarmed. They were everywhere. We barely got out of the parking lot. I sped home, but there was an accident. We got hit by a truck. Another car hit him, then another hit that one. It was so bad. I managed to get out and was reaching for Drake when one of those...things...grabbed him. I threw my arms around it and in the struggle..." She motioned her arm. "I managed to get my gun out and shot it. Then we ran home. I called you because I knew you could..." She faltered, her eyes straying to Drake. "And now you're here..." His mother burst into sobs, her body shaking. "Josh, oh, Josh, I'm so glad you're okay."

Resisting the urge to throw his arms around her, Josh reached out and gently touched her hand. She clutched it tightly. Her hand was hot and moist.

"Mom, we need to get you to the community center and a doctor."

"Josh," Lynette started, then hesitated. Her mouth twitched as she struggled to speak through her tears, fear and emotions. "Josh," she continued, her voice cracking. "I need you to take your brother and get him to a safe place. That is why I called you."

"Mom!"

"I know you can do it, Josh. If anyone on this earth can deal with this, it's you. All those movies, books, comics...everything, Josh. You know more about this than any of us." She held up her arm. "We both know what this means. I can *feel* what it is doing to me inside."

Josh felt tears pouring down his face and an ugly lump filled his throat making it hard to swallow, breathe, or talk. He swallowed hard, then said, "Those were just movies!"

"I can feel it, Josh," his mother whispered. She pressed her hand to her chest. "I feel it here. What it's doing." Her dimming blue eyes flicked to Drake. "Save your brother, Josh."

Rubbing his eyes, Josh sobbed, "What will you do?"

Her fingers lightly touched the gun at her waist. "What I have to."

"Mom, no, Mom," Josh exclaimed, falling to his knees before her.

Drake turned around, distracted from his

playing, and began to watch them.

"Take care of your brother until your dad gets back. You can do this for me. Tell your dad I love him and I will see him again someday. Please."

"Mom, I can't. I'm just a kid!"

"You're the best kid I've ever known, Josh. Do this for me. Promise me!" Lynette grabbed his hand again. This time her fingers felt cooler.

Josh looked at the pale hand clutching him. Her fingers were tinged with blue and purple. The veins stood out starkly against her white skin. Looking up at her, he saw that her eyes were even cloudier than before. Horrified, he realized how much she looked like a zombie already. His mother was dying right before his eyes.

"Do this for me," his mother said again in a faint voice. "Save your brother and yourself. Your dad will come back for both of you."

Afraid, Josh nodded. He overcame his fear of her appearance and pressed a quick, hard kiss to her cheek. It was cooler than he thought it would be. She hugged him briefly, then pushed him away.

"Go now."

"No!" Drake said firmly. "Want Mama, not Josh!" The little boy flung himself at his mother.

Josh grabbed for him, managing to catch his collar. Drake grabbed hold of Lynette's wounded arm, making her scream.

"Let go!"

"Want Mama!"

"Take him," Lynette gasped, slumping down on the couch, resting on her elbow. Blood was bubbling from her lips. "It's almost over and I have to...do....this..." Her hand gripped the gun at her waist.

Pulling with all his might, Josh managed to pry Drake off of his mother. "Leave her alone!"

"Mama, Josh is being mean. I want to be with *you*!"

"Go with Josh, Drake. I want you to go with Josh. I'm sick, Drake. I can't go with you." Lynette fumbled with the safety on the gun. Her voice was raspier, her breath coming faster.

The three year old became a tornado of limbs

flying everywhere. He twisted and jerked his body, his feet kicking. “No! No! Mama! I want to stay with Mama!”

Josh held on as tight as he could, dragging Drake to the door. It was hard to breathe and his tears kept blinding him. He had always thought it would be so cool for zombies to come and for him and his family to fight them off. He had never imagined his mom being bitten.

“Mama!” Drake screamed so loud it made Josh’s head hurt.

Reaching the door to the study, Josh pushed the door open and fought to get the squirming, kicking child through the doorway. “Mom, I’ll do it. I’ll take care of him,” he promised.

With one more hard yank, he got Drake through. He reached into the room to grab hold of the door knob when he saw his mother sit up sharply on the sofa.

“Mom, I love you, “Josh he said. “I’ll make sure Drake is safe.”

Her only response was to open her mouth,

screech, and lurch off the sofa toward him, one hand thrust out to grab him.

CHAPTER 14

Josh froze for a second, his hand still reaching for the door knob. The creature in front of him resembled his mother, but the horrible shriek that emanated from its blue lips and milky eyes meant only one thing.

"Want Mama!" Drake declared, trying to dart past Josh.

Catching his younger brother, Josh was released from his paralysis. In seconds, his mind processed that he couldn't hold his brother back and close the door at the same time with the zombie swiftly moving toward them. He quickly made his choice.

Lifting his little brother off the ground, Josh ran down the hallway toward the archway that led into the dining room. Behind him, he could hear the hard clap of his mother's boots against the wood floor. She wasn't as fast as the zombies at the school, but she was close behind him.

Drake cried, his arms flung out toward his mother, his eyes squeezed shut, his mouth open in a wail that didn't seem to end. He was heavy, but adrenaline fueled his older brother's flight across the small dining room.

Risking a few precious seconds, Josh reached out with one hand, snagged the back of one of the big wooden dining room chairs and sent it crashing to the floor behind him. The shriek of the zombie was cut off abruptly as it tripped and slammed into the floor face first.

The child gate guarded the door to the kitchen. There was no way he could leap over it holding his younger brother, so Josh tossed the three year old over the barricade. Drake landed on his side and burst into even louder cries. Josh scrambled over the gate, feeling the faint brush of his zombified mother's hand against his ankle. Snagging Drake's arm, he dragged him, hitting the door to the laundry room at full steam. He wrenched it open and pushed Drake through before following.

As he pulled the door shut, he saw the zombie that had been his mother trying to get over the child gate, the gun still clutched in her hand. She toppled over the gate head first, slamming into the kitchen floor. The gun fired with a sharp crack, the bullet slamming into the wall near Josh.

"Crap!" Josh slammed the door shut and turned to see his brother laying on the floor sobbing.

"Mama, Mama," Drake wailed.

Pulling the curtain slightly away from the window next to the back door, Josh looked into the backyard. It was peaceful. The high fence and locked gate had kept the zombie chaos from flowing over onto their property. The boughs of the oak tree that sheltered his tree house were swaying in the winds of the oncoming storm. The sky was now completely gray and threatening rain.

The door behind him began to tremble as the zombie on the other side began to beat against it. Terrified that the gun would go off again, Josh dragged Drake into his arms. His mother had said they needed to go somewhere safe until his dad could get them. The only place he could think of was his tree house.

"Drake, stop crying!"

"Mama!" Drake whimpered, thrusting his hand toward the door. "Mama!"

The sound of his voice made their zombified mother growl and slam her body against the door to the laundry room. Josh pulled open the back door and stumbled down the steps into the backyard, struggling with his brother. Drake's desperate attempts to get free sent them both sprawling onto the ground.

"You're mean!" Drake exclaimed. He began to crawl away from Josh, sobbing.

Josh leaped to his feet, turned and dashed back

up the steps. He heard the gun go off again. He gasped, terrified. It sounded like his dead mother was using the gun to try to break through the laundry room door. Reaching into the house, he felt his heart skipping in his chest. It hurt to breathe. He kept blinking sweat and tears from his eyes as he tried to focus. Gripping the doorknob, he pulled the door shut, blocking out the sound of the zombie desperately trying to pursue them.

Turning, he saw Drake lying facedown on the ground weeping. A soft rain was just beginning, dotting Drake's yellow shirt with wet spots. Josh reached down and hooked his hands under his brother's armpits.

"No! No! Want Mama," Drake sobbed. "Want Mama. Want Rex."

Lifting his brother off the ground, Josh fought down an enormous sob building up in his chest. "Mama isn't Mama anymore. She's a monster."

Drake threw back his head, sobbing.

"Yeah, yeah. Mama got sick from the monster bite," Josh explained. "She's a monster now."

Drake whimpered, all the fight going out of him. Josh assumed that his three year old mind was trying to cope with the situation.

"Want Rex," Drake finally said.

"We'll get him later," Josh promised.

He felt Drake go limp in his arms as he carried him over to the tree house. The rain started to come down at a faster pace. The world seemed eerily silent except for the gentle patter of the rain against the leaves. He couldn't even hear the sound of his dead mother pounding on the door inside the house.

"Drake, climb up."

"I can't go into the tree house," Drake whispered. "Mama and Daddy said so."

"You can this time," Josh assured him as he lifted the little boy onto the ladder.

Positioning himself directly below and slightly behind Drake, he carefully guided the little fellow up the trunk of the tree.

"I'm scared," his brother whispered as they climbed higher.

"It's okay. I'm right behind you. I got you."

Drake's small fingers shook as he gripped the rough wood nailed into the trunk. Josh moved up closer to him, pressing his chest against his brother's rear.

"It's okay, Drake. We're almost there."

Josh worried his brother would freeze on the ladder like Roger had the first time he tried to climb to the tree house, but Drake reached up for the next rung.

Together, they reached the top just as the dark clouds above released dark, cool rain down on the town. Drake crawled into the shelter and over to the makeshift sofa made up of pillows and old blankets. He fell onto it, tucking his thumb into his mouth. Josh followed him in, shaking the rain from his hair. Reaching up, he unrolled the thick, black plastic door he had made for the tree house. It hooked onto two nails at the bottom of the door. If zombies learned to climb, it wouldn't be much protection, but Josh felt confident in the sturdy gate and fence around the house.

He pulled down the old shade his dad had installed over the window and sat down beside his brother. Silent tears streamed down both their faces. He wasn't sure if it was good or bad that Drake understood that Lynette was no longer really their mother.

Dropping his head into his hands, he let out a low, shuddering sob. His heart was still pounding in his chest. His legs and arms ached from his mad dash to get to get home, and his subsequent escape from the house. If he hadn't arrived in time, he realized he would have lost his brother, too. It was too awful to think about and he let out another hiccupping sob.

He wasn't sure how long they stayed quietly crying as the storm erupted overhead, but finally his heartbeat returned to normal. His chest still felt tight and his body was aching, but he felt calmer.

Beside him, Drake dozed, thumb in his mouth. It was probably better that he slept for awhile. Josh needed time to make his next plan. If his dad didn't show up, it would be up to Josh to get them both to safety. Where that would be, he wasn't sure. His friends were probably at the community center by now. If real life followed the movies, it wouldn't be safe there for long. People who had bites would be there and soon it would get really bad.

The thought of his mother's bite and her death brought fresh, hot tears to his eyes. She had been so beautiful in life. To see her as a monstrous and terrifying zombie had been the worst thing he had ever experienced in his young life. Sadly, he had a feeling it wouldn't be the last horrible thing he would ever see.

Now he felt stupid for ever liking zombies. It had been dumb to think they were cool and fantasize about surviving the zombie apocalypse. Looking around his tree house at his idea of survival gear made him want to throw up. He had been such a stupid little kid. How his dad had trusted him to take care of his family, he didn't understand. He was just a dumb kid.

Drake murmured softly in his sleep, his fingers twitching. Josh felt bad that he hadn't snagged Rex on the way out of the house. The stupid toy would have probably comforted his brother. When Drake woke up, Josh didn't know how he was going to take care of him.

He felt utterly helpless.

And then he heard the screams.

At first he thought it was just the rain and the thunder, but then the voices rose above the wind. It took him a few more seconds to realize that the voices were calling out his name.

Scrambling to the window, he looked over the fence toward the street. Surprise filled him as he saw his friends running through the rain toward his house. Leaning out of the window, he began to shout at them as he waved.

"The backyard! I'm back here! The tree house!"

All of them raced toward his house: Troy, Roger, Arturo, Sam, little Yessica, and to his surprise, Corina. They were yelling and motioning to him.

"Go to the back gate! The back gate!" he shouted, and then he saw why they were running with such terrified expressions on their faces.

They were being chased by zombified preschoolers around Drake's age.

"Oh, crap," Josh exclaimed. "Oh, crap!"

CHAPTER 15

Tossing a worried look at his little brother, Josh was relieved to see that Drake was still asleep. Pushing aside the black plastic, Josh quickly lowered himself onto the ladder.

"Josh! Josh!" he heard his friends' frantic voices cry out.

As he climbed down, he could see them dashing through the neighbor's front yard, heading toward the path to the backyard. The gruesome zombie children behind them slashed at the air, desperate to grab hold of the fresh meat.

Josh gasped as Sam was snagged by a small girl, but the boy immediate slammed her into a tree, knocking her off. The big kid's face was bright red as he gasped for air.

Josh jumped the last few feet to the soggy ground and ran to the back gate. The rain splatted against his face as his cold fingers fumbled with the lock and latch. He could hear the footfalls of his approaching friends and the zombies.

"Open it!" It was Corina's voice. Fear filled it.

Josh's fingers shook as adrenaline spiked through his system, spurring him on. He pulled the metal spike out of the mechanism, unlocking it, and then pushed the latch up and over. He groaned as the latch caught.

The sound of something big landing in the bushes next to him made him scream and jump back from the gate.

"Open it!" Corina screamed.

Troy pulled himself out of the bushes, scratched up and bleeding, then rushed over to help get the gate open.

“It’s stuck!” Josh called out, desperately shoving on the latch.

“They’re coming!”

Yessica was lifted up over the top of the fence by Corina and Troy rushed to catch her.

“Get her, get her!” Corina ordered.

Arturo grunted as he tried to scale the wood fence, too.

“They’re gonna get Sam!” Roger shouted. “They’re gonna get him!”

“Shut up!” Sam screamed back.

“You’re going to get all the zombies coming after us!” Josh’s fingers kept slipping as he tried to get the metal bar unstuck. “Don’t push on the gate, Corina!”

She released her hold on the other side and the metal rod back slid back with a satisfying *snick*. Josh pulled the gate open as Corina shoved it. Reaching back, she grabbed Roger and hurled him inside. Sam struggled into the alley, pushing the girl zombie away from him again with his book bag.

“Someone help me! I’m stuck!” Arturo called out, draped halfway over the fence, kicking his legs.

“Run, Sam!” Corina screamed.

Josh looked around him, spotted the garden rake leaning against the fence, and grabbed it. Stepping out into the alley, he shoved the little girl zombie off her feet as she tried to leap at Sam again. Sam huffed past him toward the gate.

“Hit her again!” Corina cried out.

Another zombie rounded the corner and lunged toward Josh. Instead of swinging the rake, Josh used it to shove the boy zombie off its feet onto the little girl. The two zombified children struggled with each other as they tried to get back up.

More children turned the corner, snarling and growling. Their mutilated faces and shredded clothes were covered in blood. Josh darted back through the gate and Corina slammed it shut.

“Lock it! Lock it!” Sam cried out on the edge of hysterics.

Josh slid the bolt home then fumbled with the rod that fit into the lock to keep it secure.

“Help me!” Arturo flailed about on the top of the fence. “My belt is caught!”

Troy and Roger grabbed each grabbed one of his hands and pulled. Arturo screamed and the brothers grunted. On the other side of the fence, the zombies moaned and howled. The sturdy fence held firm despite the chaos.

While he locked the gate, Josh felt it shaking under his fingers. He put his shoulder against it, afraid it would fly open. The zombie kids on the other side slammed their hands against it while others tried to grab Arturo’s kicking legs.

Yessica sat on the swing of the playscape taking yet another hit on her inhaler. Sam stared at the gate, his mouth gapping open, breathing heavily. Corina punched his arm and motioned to a wheelbarrow.

“Get that. We need to barricade the gate.”

Sam shook himself out of his daze. She pointed at the wheelbarrow again, and he hurried to get it.

“I think it will hold just fine,” Josh said, the steady smack of small hands on the other side making the thick wood gate vibrate.

Arturo let out a loud shriek as the brothers finally yanked him down. His legs came over his head as he went down, his belt breaking. His jeans ended up around his ankles as he tumbled into the bushes and into an empty flowerbed. Any other day it would have been funny, but the blood running down his tan legs terrified all the kids looking at his predicament.

Pulling his jeans up as fast as he could, Arturo glowered at all of them. "They almost got me!"

"Did they get you?" Josh demanded.

"No! I got all cut up falling off your stupid fence!" Arturo fumbled with his broken belt before hurling it into the trees. "This whole day is stupid!"

Corina and Sam shoved the wheelbarrow against the fence as Josh stepped away. Corina began pulling up the rocks that lined the dead garden, piling them into the wheelbarrow to weigh it down. Sam immediately began to help her.

Josh stepped in front of Arturo, looking his best friend straight in the eye. "Dude, if you're bitten, we need to know."

"I'm not, okay? I got hurt coming over the fence!"

Troy looked warily at Josh as Roger sat down beside Yessica. "I think we better check him."

"Leave me alone!" Arturo said crossly. With a frown etched on his forehead, he began to stalk across the yard toward the house.

"You can't go in there!" Josh called after him.

"They didn't bite me!"

"But they bit my mom," Josh answered, his voice catching in his throat. "They bit my mom and she's...she's..." He felt fresh tears roll down his cheeks.

"Oh, man." Troy reached out and laid his hand on Josh's shoulder. "Oh, man, Josh..." Troy, too, struggled with tears, remembering his own father's death.

"They're just sick," Roger said after a beat. "Zombies aren't real, they're make believe. It's like *28 Days Later*. They're gonna get a cure and it's gonna be okay. Really."

"Don't be stupid," Sam snorted.

"I'm not!"

"Don't call Rog stupid! It's your lard butt that almost got us killed!" Arturo hissed back.

"Stop fighting!" Corina ordered. It was her best babysitter voice and the boys lapsed into silence. "Stop it! It's not doing any good. And I think it's making them try harder to get us." She pointed at the quivering gate and stepped away from it. "Is your mom very sick? Do you think we could just lock her in her bedroom, Josh?"

"She's already one of them," Josh answered. "We can't go in. She's in the kitchen. She still has a gun in her hand. She was going to...you know...but she...she just got so sick and then she was a zombie."

"Zombies aren't real," Roger said simply.

"Shut up, Rog," Troy commanded. "Drop it."

"But they're not real! Those people are sick! Like *28*-"

"Lame," Sam huffed.

"Look, lardo, you're the one who said we should

go to city hall, and we almost got killed. We barely made it here!"

"My dad has his office there. He would protect us!"

"The sheriff wasn't at the community center, Arturo. Going to get him to help us was a good idea. It wasn't a bad plan," Corina said firmly, defending Sam.

"Until we ran into the preschoolers from hell!"

"Don't swear, Arturo." Troy ran a hand over his Afro, obviously trying to think.

From above them came a hiccuping cry that immediately grew louder.

"It's Drake. He woke up," Josh explained. "Come up."

He quickly scrambled up the ladder and pushed back the black flap. Drake was lying on his side sobbing loudly.

"Are you a monster?"

"No, Drake. I'm okay. So are my friends. They're coming up."

"I hear monsters."

"They can't get into the yard. We're safe," Josh promised as he sat next to Drake.

Yessica climbed in, looking around, followed closely by Corina. They moved onto a pile of pillows near Drake. They were both wet from the rain and flushed. Josh couldn't help but stare at Corina. She looked older and beautiful despite her glasses being slightly bent on her face.

Arturo climbed in and retreated to his usual corner where he promptly unrolled his Spider-Man sleeping bag. Roger followed, his complexion much paler than usual. Troy slid in and the brothers took up their usual position on a platform built up higher on the branches. It was like a deep shelf and they liked sitting there. Sam was last. His beet-red face appeared at the doorway, his hands trembling from exertion.

"He can't fit his fat gut in here. He's gonna have to stay outside," Arturo decided.

"Shut up, Arturo. He can make it," Corina said crossly.

"C'mon, Sam," Yessica urged.

Exhaustion, his weight, and his fear of heights worked against Sam. He hung onto the edges of the doorway breathing heavily. "I won't fit."

"Yeah, you will," Corina assured him. She scooted over a little, opening up an area for him to sit near the window.

"What if I make it fall?"

"My dad built this. It's sturdy. I promise. He had his buddies up here one night playing poker. It's not going to fall," Josh promised.

Finally, Sam pulled his gut over the edge of the floor and crawled inside. He immediately fell over into his corner, panting.

Josh pulled the black plastic back into the place and the children sat in silence. The rain had moved on without them noticing and the wind had died down. The tree limbs moaned along with the children down in the alley.

"We should be quiet," Corina said in a low voice. "They're quieter now that they can't see us."

Spent of all their energy and overwhelmed by the day's events, it was easy for the Zombie Hunters and their guests to fall into silence. Even Drake was quiet; sucking on his thumb as Josh gently rubbed his back.

Sam reached out and lowered the blinds over the window, blocking out the view from the front of the house and side yard. The tree house was enveloped in the gloom of the late afternoon.

Drake began to doze off again, as did Roger. Sam's heaving breathing finally calmed down and his face wasn't so red anymore. Corina slid off the pillows to let Yessica lie down and moved to sit cross-legged next to Josh. In the corner, Arturo was buried under his sleeping bag, out of sight. Troy sat with his back to the wall, his knees up to his chest, staring off into space. He was silently crying.

Josh didn't blame him.

Gently, Corina touched Josh's hand and he looked toward her. Her eyes slid toward Arturo, her expression tense.

"What is it?" he asked in a hushed tone.

Cupping her hand against his ear, Corina leaned against him, her lips brushing his ear as she whispered, “I saw Arturo’s leg. A zombie bit him.”

Josh swallowed. Slowly, he looked toward his best friend huddled in the corner.

Her hand trembling and her voice ragged, she said, “We’re going to have to kill him.”

CHAPTER 16

Josh had not ever dared dream of being this close to Corina, and he felt a flutter inside his belly he had never felt before.

Turning his head slightly toward her, he whispered back, "Are you sure?"

She nodded solemnly, her eyes huge behind her glasses.

They both looked at Arturo. They could barely see the top of his head poking out over the edge of his sleeping bag. His mussed hair had flecks of dirt and grass still clinging to it.

Josh wasn't sure how long the bite that had turned his mother had taken to do its damage. She had been bleeding pretty steadily from the wound. There were a few drops of blood on the tree house floor, but not nearly as much as he had seen dripping from his mother's bite. Maybe Arturo really had scraped up his legs going over the fence. His pants had been pulled all the way down to his ankles when he had fallen.

Finally, with a weary sigh, Josh turned his attention back to Corina and said in a low voice, "We have to be sure."

Troy slid off the upper portion of the tree house and squatted down beside them. His Afro was lopsided from him running his hands over it and beads of sweat decorated his flushed cheeks. His dark eyes examined their worried expressions, then he turned his attention to Arturo. He motioned toward his friend, arching an eyebrow.

Josh nodded.

Corina drew back her lips and took an imaginary

bite out of the air.

Troy dropped his head into his hands and sighed.

"The zombie really got him?" Sam exclaimed in terror. "Oh, my God! Are you going to kill him?"

"Sam!" Corina chastised him.

Arturo yanked down the edge of the sleeping bag and glowered at Sam. "Not funny, turd head."

"She says you got a bite for real!" Sam scrambled to his feet, breathing heavily. Fear had a good grip on him.

Yessica stirred as Drake slept on. Roger slowly sat up, blinking. With his half-closed eyes and slack expression, he looked drugged.

"Keep your voice down," Josh said firmly, but in a low voice. "The zombies are quiet now. Don't ruin it."

Sam bit his bottom lip and slowly sat down again. He curled his body up against the wall, staring at Arturo fearfully.

Arturo grumbled, trying to get comfortable again.

Josh slowly crawled over to his best friend and sat down beside him. "Arturo, did you get a bite?"

"No! I got hurt falling over your stupid fence. Leave me alone already." Anger filled his voice, but fear tinged his features. His dark green eyes were averted and he was shivering slightly.

"Dude, if you're bit, we gotta...you know...you'll end up one of those things."

"No, I won't. I didn't get a bite. I got hurt falling. And...and...we're best friends, Josh. You wouldn't hurt me," Arturo insisted. His voice was ragged with emotion. "Gawd, Josh, everything is all messed up and I'm scared. I don't need you ragging on me 'cause I busted up my legs."

Embarrassed by his friend's tears, Josh rested a hand on his shoulder. "It's okay, dude. I got your back."

"Do you?"

"Yeah. Always."

"But he'll be a zombie!" Sam protested. "He'll try to eat us!"

"I don't wanna get eated," Drake said sleepily.

"No one is going to eat you," Corina assured Drake as she moved to his side to comfort him.

Despite Josh's best effort to diffuse the situation, it was clear that Corina did not believe Arturo. Her jaw was set and her lips pressed into a thin line. She busied herself tucking in the two youngest children.

Rubbing his head, Troy said, "Arturo, maybe we should look."

"Screw you," Arturo answered. "Josh believes me and he's my best friend. Back off."

"Let him be, Troy." Josh looked at Troy significantly, hoping he would understand he needed to let it go for now. They would have to watch Arturo carefully, but getting him upset would only make matters worse.

Troy studied the expressions of both Arturo and Josh, then shrugged. Without a word, he climbed back up onto the higher level and settled down next to his brother.

Roger yawned and looked around a bit dazed. "We should go home, Troy."

"No way. I'm not going down there with the zombies again," Troy said firmly.

"Mom and Dad will be worried," Roger continued.

"Dad is dead and we don't know where Mom is. She wasn't at the community center."

"What did happen at the community center? Why aren't you guys there?" Josh asked, suddenly curious.

"It got bad there," Corina answered. "They were bringing in lots of people with really bad bites. There were some doctors there from the Army or something. They kept the people with bites over in another room and the rest of us were in that big room where they have all the weddings."

"My mommy and daddy weren't there," Yessica sighed.

"Neither was my mom." Arturo sniffled. "I miss her."

"None of our parents were there. No one even really paid attention to us," Corina explained. "So we hung out in the back near the kitchen."

"Yeah, then the zombies started eating people," Sam said sullenly.

"We think that was what was happening. We heard screaming from that room where all the bite victims were with the doctors," Corina explained.

"So we took off," Arturo said sullenly.

"Yeah, the other people were stupid and ran to where all the screaming was coming from," Sam said grumpily.

"Zombie food," Troy decided.

Corina shoved her glasses up on her nose as she settled back down on the pillows. "We ran away through the back door. Sam thought about trying to find his dad, so we started to go to City Hall when we saw those kids in the distance."

"I didn't know they were zombies," Yessica said softly.

"It's not your fault," Corina smoothed Yessica wild curls. "It's okay."

"Yessica waved at them," Troy sighed.

"They came after us, so we started running," Arturo continued. "We decided to come here because we thought your mom could maybe help us."

"That was fail," Troy muttered.

"Yeah, 'cause your mom is a zombie," Sam explained.

Josh winced, trying not to let Sam's comment get to him. "So the community center is wiped out?"

Corina nodded. "I'm pretty sure."

"Adults are dumb. They always do the wrong thing, just like in the movies." Troy shook his head. "Just like the movies."

Roger sat next to his brother, his head down, looking like he was walking in his sleep. Josh was worried about him. It was obvious Roger was not taking the situation well at all. None of them were, of course, but Roger didn't seem to comprehend what was really going on.

"Troy, we should call mom," Roger insisted after a long pause in the conversation.

"Do you still have my cellphone?" Josh felt a thrill of hope. If he could call his dad and let him know where they were, he could come rescue them.

"Yeah." Troy fished it out of his pocket. "I tried to call my mom on it, but she didn't answer."

Josh grabbed it and quickly scrolled through the menu to find his dad's cellphone number. He hit the button, listening to it dial then a woman's voice told him all the circuits were busy and to try again later.

"Crap," he groaned. "It's not working."

"Let me try my mom." Corina took the phone, dialed, and listened. After a few minutes, she clicked the button to hang up. "It's just ringing and she doesn't have a cellphone." Tears sparkled in her eyes as she stared at the phone.

"You live right next door. Maybe if you yell loud enough she'll come to the window," Sam suggested.

Corina shook her head. "She was at work and the car isn't there. I looked when we ran past." Her voice was rough with emotion. Josh knew she was wondering if her mother was even still alive.

Arturo held out his hand for the phone, so Corina passed it over. She narrowed her eyes as he took it, obviously suspicious of his condition. Arturo dialed his number and waited. His eyes reddened as the phone rang on the other end. Without a word, he passed the phone on to Roger and turned his face toward the wall. He was obviously trying to contain his tears.

His hands slightly shaking, Roger dialed and listened. Finally, in a quivering voice he said, “Mom, come get us at Josh’s. We’re in the tree house.”

Troy sat up sharply, hope springing into his features. “Mom? You’re talking to Mom?”

Roger shook his head as he hung up. “Voice mail. But she’ll hear it when she gets home and come get us.”

His shoulders slumping, Troy sat back against the wall.

Sam scrambled over Yessica to grab the phone from Roger.

“Hey!” Yessica pushed him off her.

“I need to call my dad!”

“Me, too!” Yessica punched his arm.

“You’ll go next,” Corina promised Yessica giving Sam the stink eye.

Sam ignored her and started to breathe heavily as he dialed. He obviously misdialed once or twice and had to start over. His fingers trembled with fear and excitement. He raised the phone to his ear and listened. Rubbing his lips together, Sam rocked himself as he waited.

The sound of the busy signal was so loud, they all heard it.

Sam hung up and dialed again. "Trying my mom."

This time Sam listened to the phone ringing until Corina finally took the phone away from him. Silently, she handed it to Yessica.

The little girl dialed carefully, mouthing the numbers as she punched the buttons. Bringing the phone to her ear, she looked at the other children with fear in her eyes. Those eyes suddenly widened as she whispered, "Daddy?"

Josh could hear a man's voice answer her.

"Daddy! Daddy! I'm not a zombie! I'm safe!"

All the kids surged forward, straining to hear the voice of the adult.

"I'm with some other kids. The bus crashed and there were zombies and they tried to eat us. They ate Mary." Yessica's bottom lip trembled as tears formed in her eyes. "Uh huh. I'm safe. I'm in a tree house. On a cellphone. Some boy's. Uh...where am I?"

"483 West Current Street," Josh answered her quickly.

Yessica slowly repeated the address, Josh correcting her when she messed up. "No. We're just kids. Nobody is grownup. When Daddy? Okay! Okay!"

Josh snatched the phone away from her, unable to wait. "Hi, this is Josh Rondell. Are you coming for us, sir?"

"I'm on foot, kid. I'm hiding in a tool shed right now," the man's voice said in hushed tones. "I'll come for you as soon as I can. Keep Yessica safe, okay? I need to go. I'm afraid they're gonna hear me."

As the line went dead, Josh looked up at the other children gathered around him. Yessica was tucked into Corina's arms crying softly with relief.

"He's going to come as soon as he can," Josh

said. “He’s holed up like we are, but when he can, he’ll come for us.”

“Then we’re saved!” Sam declared.

“Ssshhh,” Corina reminded him.

“If he can find a vehicle and get here, yeah, we’re totally saved,” Josh said with relief.

“And if he doesn’t?” Troy dared to ask.

“My dad will get us,” Josh promised. “He will.”

Josh looked down at the small, cheap cellphone. He kept hoping his dad would call. But if Yessica’s dad could help them get to a safer place, maybe his dad could join them there. He hoped Yessica’s dad stayed safe.

From across the tree house, Arturo let out a low moan.

The children froze.

CHAPTER 17

"Arturo?" Josh looked around for a weapon, fear gripping him tight, making his stomach twist into a knot.

His best friend's face was turned toward the wall.

"Are you a zombie?" Sam blurted out.

"Zombies aren't real, stupid," Roger responded. His voice still sounded odd and slightly off key.

Arturo looked over his shoulder at the other kids, his eyes rimmed with red, fresh tears brimming. "I'm not a zombie! My leg hurts and I miss my mom!" Arturo shouted. "Leave me alone, losers!"

Josh felt relieved for a second, but then the zombies in the alley began to moan loudly and beat on the fence again.

"Shhh, all of you," Corina whispered urgently. "We can't be too loud."

"I'm thirsty." Drake rubbed his eyes and, staring at his brother. "I want water."

"Me, too." Yessica looked pale and tired. Dry blood stained her clothes and her hair was a mess of tangles.

Josh crawled over to the ice chest in the corner and popped the lid. There was no ice, but water bottles were lined up inside. He handed out the warm drinks, each kid passing the bottles to the next child on until they all had one. Corina helped Drake open his, then gulped down her own.

"I'm hungry," Sam complained. "My stomach hurts I'm so hungry."

"Of course you are." Arturo glowered at the boy.

"I'm hungry, too." Troy slid off his perch and began to rummage through all the snacks they had stored in the hollow of the tree.

"We need to ration out the food just in case we have to wait awhile," Josh decided. "So everyone just eat a little, okay?"

Corina popped open a small can of Vienna sausages and handed one to Drake. "Everyone eat something with meat in it. Not just sugar stuff."

"Yes, Mom," Troy answered sarcastically.

"Don't call her mom. She's not our mom. Our mom is coming to get us," Roger exclaimed, but remembered to at least keep his voice down.

"It was a joke, bro." Troy tossed Roger a small bag of chips and a small can of ravioli.

"What do you want Arturo?" Josh held up some single serving cans of soup, ravioli and chili.

"Nothing. I'm not hungry. And my stomach hurts. When I was hanging on the fence it got all mashed up." Arturo pulled his sleeping bag up higher around his face.

Josh realized his friend was shivering. He looked back at Corina, his expression etched with worry. She slowly chewed her own food before handing

Drake and Yessica another sausage. Sighing, she nodded her head and mouthed the word "Bitten." Arturo didn't see the movement, but the other kids did.

"You can't kill Arturo," Roger suddenly shouted. "You can't kill him, Josh!"

"Whoa! Who said I was going to kill him?"

"This is stupid! I'm not a zombie!" Arturo protested.

"I'm not going to kill him! Why would you say that?" Josh demanded.

"You killed my dad!" Roger screamed.

Troy slapped his hand over his brother's mouth. "Dude, Dad was a zombie."

Roger struggled against Troy, his eyes wide over his brother's fingers.

"I just meant to trip him so we could get away," Josh explained, rubbing his hands against his knees. He didn't want to add in the part where he had planned to hit their zombie father over the head with his stick. "My plan just worked better than I thought."

With some effort, Roger yanked his brother's hand away from his mouth. "You killed him! You can't kill Arturo!"

"I'm not a zombie!"

The groans of the zombies grew even louder outside as the kids' voices rose. They began to bang their fists against the fence and gate again.

"Everyone, shush!" Corina pointed her finger in Arturo's face then in Roger's. "Enough already. We don't need those things getting into the yard. We need to stay safe until we get rescued."

Looking up from the corner from where he was hungrily eating a bag of chips, Sam said in a loud whisper, "When they come get us, they can just shoot the zombies with guns."

"My daddy doesn't have a gun," Yessica informed him.

"But my dad does. He'll come for us once I get a hold of him."

"We need to go home," Roger said to his brother in a softer voice. "Mom is going to be worried."

"Rog, just shut up." Troy shoved a bag of chips

into Roger's hand. "Eat."

Josh shook his head, trying to get his thoughts together. His friends were starting to get on his nerves. He wanted to yell at Sam that his dad was probably dead, scream at Roger that his mom was probably a zombie, and demand that Arturo show them his leg. Instead, he got up and peeked around the edge of the plastic doorway.

The small zombies were not visible from his location, but he could see some adult zombies wandering through the yards of the houses behind his. Drawing away from the doorway, he frowned. There were no other living people visible. The sun was beginning to set and he began to worry about Yessica's dad finding them in the dark.

Crawling over to the window, he pulled back the shade a little and looked out toward the front of the house. There were a few zombies in the front yard. They appeared disoriented as they wandered in circles or stood staring up at the sky.

"Okay, we have minimal zombies right now. We got the dead kids in the alley and some adults wandering around, but not like a massive amount. This is good. But we got to keep it quiet. Maybe if we're quiet enough they will go away." Josh settled down near the door and opened up a can of spaghetti. He fished a plastic spoon out of a bag they had in their stash and started to eat. Despite being cold, it was delicious.

Corina finished eating and began collecting all the trash. She stuffed it into the pillow case she stripped off one of the pillows and hung it from a nail. Then, as the others ate, she began organizing the sleeping bags and pillows into sleeping areas for the little kids.

Josh couldn't help but watch her. She was so pretty and strong compared to most girls. She even had Drake quieted down and obeying her. She got the two small kids to share a makeshift bed with her in the middle of the tree house by handing them toys off the shelves to play with.

Josh tossed his trash into the makeshift trash bag and restacked the food in the hollow of the trunk. Troy and Roger sat up in their area whispering in soft voices. It was obvious they were disagreeing, but they kept it down.

It was growing darker and darker inside the tree house. Josh knew that soon they would be in total darkness. His gaze strayed to the flashlight he used to read when in the clubhouse at night. Reaching up, he snagged it. It was big and heavy. His dad had carried it during the war.

It was hard to swallow at the thought of his dad. Josh didn't want to let him down, but he feared he was. His mother was dead and he didn't know how to take care of Drake. If Corina hadn't showed up, he wasn't sure he could have kept the kid calm. He was grateful Corina was with them now. When he had seen her ride off with Brad at the school, he had feared he would never see her again.

"Where is Brad?"

Corina looked at Josh, startled. "Huh?"

"Brad?"

"He left me at the community center and took off. He said he was going to go get his mom." She said all of this calmly. Her fingers made two

Transformers fight an epic battle for Drake's amusement as she spoke, but her gaze gave away her heartbreak. They both knew what had probably happened to her boyfriend, his mom, and Corina's own mother.

Josh sat with his back against the wall, his elbows resting on his knees and the flashlight heavy in his hands. This wasn't really what he had imagined the zombocalypse would be like. For one thing, he thought his dad would be with him and that they would have guns. Instead, his dad was far away, his mother was dead, and the guns were locked up. Josh had no idea where to even start to look for the key to the gun cabinets even if he could get into the house.

"I miss my mom," Arturo's muffled voice came from the depths of his sleeping bag. He was shivering so violently Josh could hear his teeth chattering. Maybe it was fear or maybe it was the zombie infection that was making Arturo's teeth click together.

Josh sympathized with Arturo's comment. He

missed his mom, too. "I wish my mom was here, too."

"Mama is a monster," Drake said softly. "I want my daddy. Mama wants to eat me."

"He'll come get you soon," Corina promised.

Yessica rubbed her nose and looked around the tree house. "It's too dark. It's scary."

"We better not turn on any lights. It might make the zombies more riled up."

"Yeah, they're quiet now." Troy tilted his head listening.

It was true. There was no more pounding or loud growls and wails. There were soft moans filling the growing stillness of the night, but it was an almost peaceful sound.

Arturo burrowed deeper into his sleeping bag, softly crying, the sound of his teeth clicking together a frightening sound.

Josh sighed and looked back toward Corina. Her gaze was on the heavy flashlight. Flicking her gaze back to Arturo, then back to the flashlight, Josh understood. It suddenly felt and looked like an instrument of death. But he didn't think he could use it as a weapon against his friend. He always thought it would be easy to kill zombies, but he hadn't expected them to be his mom and best friend.

"I'm scared of the dark," Yessica whimpered. "Please turn it on."

Aiming the flashlight at the floor, just above the wood, Josh turned it on. A small ring of light dimly illuminated the tree house. Instantly, everyone was draped in shadows and darkness. It was even more disconcerting than the deep gloom that had enveloped them as the sun set.

Corina slid off the makeshift bed to kneel next to Josh. In a soft voice she said, "I think we should sleep in shifts. Someone should always be awake, alert for either Yessica's or your dad coming to get us."

"Yeah. That sounds like a good plan."

"We're all really tired and stressed out. Sleep will be good."

Josh was mesmerized by her big brown eyes and

the way she seemed so calm when other girls would have been crying. The one thing he was sure of in life was that there weren't that many cool girls. He knew Corina was keeping them all calm and keeping the little ones from freaking out and crying. She was the coolest girl he knew and he loved her.

"Do you want to take the first shift, Josh?"

"Yeah. Yeah." He fished his cellphone out of his pocket and looked at the time.

"Wake me up in four hours?"

"Okay."

Looking around, he saw that Sam was already dozing, his mouth hanging open. Drake and Yessica still played quietly, but they both had droopy eyes. Roger and Troy were silent up in their area. Arturo was quiet in the corner.

It was not nearly as exciting as he had imagined. He had thought of the tree house as their fort, their command center. His former dreams about the zombies rising were washed away by the reality of seeing his mom become one right before his eyes.

"You're doing really good," Corina whispered to

Josh, her hand resting lightly on his arm. "You're being a good leader."

"I'm only twelve years old," he answered. "I'm just a stupid kid."

The older woman of his dreams just smiled at him and pressed a kiss to his cheek. Her hair still smelled of her shampoo and her lips were very soft. The flutter in his stomach returned as he felt his face flush deeply. She grinned and started to crawl back to where Drake and Yessica were slowly falling asleep.

Settling back against the wall next to the doorway, Josh swirled the light from the flashlight around on the floor. He considered turning it off when he hard a noise in Arturo's corner. Instinctively, he slid the beam toward his friend. The light hit Arturo square in the face, illuminating his cloudy green eyes, his snarling mouth, and bared teeth.

"Josh," Corina gasped. "He's a zombie!"

CHAPTER 18

Arturo lunged his head forward, his teeth snapping as a terrifying growl emanated from his throat. He had been tucked so deeply inside of his sleeping bag when he died, the zombie version of him was entangled in the fabric. The zombified boy struggled to free himself as he groaned. The other children woke up, their screams sending fresh terror down Josh's spine.

"Kill it!" Sam screamed in terror. "Kill it!"

Yessica and Drake began to cry as Corina shoved

them behind her.

Again, the zombified Arturo whipped his head forward, gnashing his teeth at Josh. Josh was the closest of the children to the zombie and he scooted backward away from it. Pitched too far forward, the zombie boy fell onto his face, his hands finally free of the sleeping bag and clawing at the wood floor.

Josh drew back in terror.

"Kill it!" Sam shouted. "You gotta kill it!"

"He's infected! Don't hurt him," Roger exclaimed. He began to move toward Arturo "We have to help him!"

"Shut up, Rog!" Troy angrily yanked his brother back, keeping him safely away from the zombie.

Zombie Arturo lashed out at Josh again, grabbing for his ankle. Chomping his teeth together, the creature surged forward.

"Josh!" Corina screamed.

Josh swung the flashlight as hard as he could. It impacted with the side of the zombie's head, knocking him to one side.

Corina darted forward and yanked the sleeping

bag over the zombie's head. Troy jumped onto the writhing zombie's back, trying to pin it down. Corina knelt on the small of its back as she placed her hands directly on top of the back of its head, shoving its face into the thick material of the bag and the floor. It was surprisingly strong as it bucked and struggled under the two kids.

Josh stared at the struggle, fear and disgust tangled up in his belly.

"We can't hold him down like this forever," Troy grunted. "Do something!"

Corina looked up at Josh, her fingers struggling to keep a firm grip on the zombie boy's head beneath the thick fabric of the sleeping bag. It was terrifying to see how the creature thrashed about beneath her. The zombie managed to get its face turned, its cheek to the floor. Its teeth snapped terribly close to her hand. Only the sleeping bag kept her safe from that terrible, desperate mouth.

"Josh, help me," she pleaded, her gaze flicking to the flashlight in his hand.

Swallowing hard, Josh realized what he had to

do. The ugly creature trying to get free to feast on him and his friends wasn't Arturo anymore; it wasn't his friend. It was something grotesquely twisted.

"Josh!" Corina gasped desperately as the creature began to tire her.

Troy continued to pin down the boy's legs, but he too was struggling. The undead would never be tired. But the living would grow weary.

Josh's thoughts whirled around like a tornado inside his mind before it snapped onto the only action he could really take. Grabbing one of the covers off the makeshift bed Corina had made, he flung it over the zombie's head. Lifting the flashlight high over his head, he briefly saw Corina's big eyes glistening with tears.

"On three let go."

"Okay," she whispered back.

"One..."

"Oh, man," Sam muttered, pulling Yessica and Drake over to him, making them turn their faces away.

"Two..."

"You can do it, Josh!" Troy's voice was ragged, but firm.

"Three..."

Corina yanked her hands away from the back of the zombie's head. The light left her face as he slammed down the flashlight.

Josh tried to pretend it was a watermelon under the cover. Or a cantaloupe. It wasn't really a zombie that used to be his best friend. He kept hitting the lumpy shape until the zombie stopped moving. With his final blow, the flashlight broke.

Darkness filled the tree house as the children wept for their fallen friend.

"Is he dead?" Sam's voice asked out of the darkness.

"Yeah. He's not moving anymore," Troy answered.

Josh threw the broken flashlight out the doorway of the tree house and felt his way through the dark to find the smaller one he kept up on a shelf with some zombie bobble head toys. His foot nudged

Yessica's leg and she let out a strangled cry.

"It's just me," Josh promised her.

His fingers desperately searched the shelf for the small light saber flashlight Arturo had given him for his last birthday. The blackness filling the tree house began to fray his nerves as the bobble heads fell to the floor around him, making the other children gasp. Finally, his hand closed around the cylindrical shape.

He flipped it on and light filled the tree house.

Corina still sat on the zombie's shoulders with Troy perched behind her on its legs. They were both still pressing down on the body, afraid to let go. There was no movement beneath the cover or the sleeping bag. Blood was beginning to pool around the shape's head. Fighting back tears of despair, pangs of guilt, and terrible fear, Josh knelt down and set the light saber flashlight down at his side. The light shifted, casting long shadows. He could see Roger perched on the edge of the other level staring down at him with dark eyes. His expression was unreadable.

Gripping the sleeping bag in both hands, Josh motioned for Corina and Troy to get up. They obeyed and helped him scoot the heavy burden to the doorway. Together, they pushed it out.

The body of their friend hit the ground below with a horrible *thunk*. Corina grabbed up another small blanket and began mopping up the blood.

"Arfurro was a monster," Drake whispered to Yessica.

"I know," she answered, her voice catching on her sobs.

Troy grabbed some water and an old towel someone had donated to the tree house back in the day. He helped Corina clean up the last of the blood then helped her wash off her hands. They tossed the soiled cloth out of the clubhouse.

Josh sat silently near the door, looking at the light saber flashlight. He remembered chasing Arturo around the backyard at night with it, pretending to slash at him like a Jedi. They were best friends from the first moment they met. Josh was the calm one, Arturo the smart aleck. It had worked perfectly. Now Arturo was gone just like his mom.

Just like the rest of the world.

"Listen," Sam said.

Josh raised his head, focusing his senses outward. Listening, he realized he only heard one solitary moan and a single hand beating against the fence.

"The zombies gave up," Sam decided.

"Or they found someone else to eat." Troy shrugged his shoulders and shook his head. "That's probably it."

Drake crawled into Corina's arms and cuddled up against her. He stuck his fingers back in his mouth, seeming more like a baby than he had in a long time. His former babysitter rocked him and kissed him, holding him tightly.

"He lied," Josh said finally. "About being bitten."

"Yeah," Corina agreed.

"Or maybe he was in denial." Troy rubbed his hands over his hair again.

"Or both." Sam sat back in the corner, Yessica

leaning against him. They both looked exhausted and their faces were stained from crying. "Poor Arturo."

"You didn't even like him," Troy snorted.

"No, that's not true," Sam answered defensively. "I wanted to be his friend."

Josh felt like his insides were shaking. He felt like he might throw up, but it wasn't his stomach that was quivering; it was his heart. Deep inside, he knew he had done something he would never forget. Even though he had killed a monster, he couldn't feel proud of himself.

"He was my best friend," Josh said at last.

"You saved us," Corina reminded him, her fingers gently stroking Drake's blond curls. "You saved all of us, including Drake."

In his sick, quivering heart, Josh knew his dad would be proud of him. His dad would cry with him over Arturo's loss, but would tell him that he had done the right thing. That he had been a good soldier.

"We should sleep," Josh decided. "Four hour

shifts."

"I'll go after you," Corina offered.

Troy climbed back up next to his sullen brother. "I'll go after her."

"I'll go after Troy." Sam settled into the corner, sitting up, pillows behind his back.

Yessica leaned back against his beefy side and he didn't shove her away. They almost looked like brother and sister.

Corina lay down with Drake. Josh noticed her hands were shaking. Looking down, he saw his were, too.

"I love you, Josh," Drake said unexpectedly, holding out his arms.

"I love you, too, lil' bro," Josh answered. He crawled over to his brother and hugged him.

"I need to poop," Drake informed him.

"Ugh!"

It took a few minutes to figure out how to do the deed. Corina held onto Drake while he hung his little butt out the window and did his business. Wet wipes that Josh's mother had insisted on him bringing up so they could clean their hands before eating snacks were used as toilet paper. As soon as Drake was done, Yessica had to go.

For the next twenty minutes, the kids had their moment of either sitting with their rear over the edge of the window or standing as they peed out of it. The boys had it easier and Corina had to help Yessica by herself while the boys stared firmly in the other direction. Roger came down long enough to pee, then immediately climbed back into his refuge.

Josh was the last to take his turn. The low moans in the night seemed far away and he felt awkward looking over the neighborhood as he relieved himself.

As he stood listening to the ordinary sounds of the night mingle with the groans and cries of the zombies, he wished with all his heart he would wake up and find out it was a dream.

CHAPTER 19

"Josh, wake up," Corina's voice said urgently.

Josh jerked awake. He had been dreaming about his dad. The details were blurred in his mind's eye, but he remembered his dad telling him that he was coming for him.

"Josh, wake up!"

"I am awake," he answered groggily.

"Listen." Corina's face was illuminated by the moonlight spilling in from the open window. She had pulled up the shade during her watch.

At first Josh wasn't sure what he was hearing, then he realized it was a motorcycle engine growling somewhere nearby. Crawling over to the window, Josh looked out into the murky darkness dwelling around the houses. The dark shapes of the undead stumbled through the front yard of Corina's house. A few zombies stood swaying under the yellow light of the sole street light on the block. The zombies turned and stared up the road toward the rumbling of the motorcycle. Slowly, they began to walk in the direction of the noise. The zombies milling around in the yards of the neighborhood shambled after them. Josh felt a shiver flow down his back as he realized they were after their next meal.

"Do you think it's Brad?" Josh asked in a soft voice, careful not to wake their friends or alert the departing zombies to their location.

"It might be. He said he'd come back for me. I think he might come to my house." Corina bit her bottom lip, her fingers gripping the edge of the window tightly.

"The zombies are all heading down the road

now." Josh furrowed his brow. "Whoever it is better take off before they get close."

The roar of the motorcycle abruptly cut off and Corina gripped Josh's arm tightly. Together they crouched by the window anxiously watching the road and surrounding area. The zombies were no longer in sight and it was a relief to not be surrounded by the undead.

A few minutes later, Brad emerged from the shadows behind Corina's house, running alongside his silent bike. He was pushing it along, his hands gripping the handlebars. Josh realized that Brad had probably killed the engine and ran up the alley once he had lured the zombies down the block.

Corina started to call out, but Josh slapped his hand over her mouth. "Don't let the zombies hear you. They'll come back."

Her eyes widened, then she nodded.

He dropped his hand.

Brad parked his motorcycle next to the rear porch of Corina's house before trying the back door only to find it locked. He moved on to a window, tapping on it lightly. They could barely hear him call out Corina's name.

"We have to let him know we're up here." Corina tugged on one of her ponytails, looking nervous.

"Okay, I'll go down and get him to climb over the fence," Josh decided. "I'll take the flashlight and signal him through the fence. If I do it from up here, the zombies might see."

They could see Brad's shadowy figure as he edged around the side of the house, stepping into the light from the street lamp. Corina let out a little gasp. It was obvious that he had been through a lot during the day. His arm was heavily bandaged and he walked with a limp. His blond hair was matted and dark with blood. At some point, his shirt had been torn. Only one sleeve remained and the torn cloth flapped around him as he moved. As he turned first one way, then the other, a terrible wound on his shoulder became visible. A large chunk of skin and flesh was missing. It looked like a bite.

Corina clamped her hands over her mouth to keep from crying out. Josh sighed heavily. He looked down at the flashlight and considered his options.

If he went down and let Brad into their safe haven and he was bitten, it would be very hard for the kids to fight off a burly sixteen year old. If Brad wasn't really bitten, it wasn't fair to leave him down there to face the zombies alone.

Picking up a brick from the crumbling walkway around Corina's home, Brad looked around one more time before slamming it into a window. The sound of the glass shattering seemed horribly loud in the stillness of the night. Brad lifted himself into the house and disappeared.

Streaks of tears marred Corina's face as she leaned her head against Josh's shoulder. She sniffled loudly, rubbing her nose.

"I can go get him," Josh said finally.

Corina motioned to Drake sleeping nearby. "We can't risk it."

"It might not be a bite."

Shaking her head, Corina sobbed, "I saw it. So did you. Something took a big piece out of him. And he looked so pale."

Josh hadn't noticed that fact, but Corina tended to be more observant than he was. He swept his hair back from his face with one hand and stared into the black void beyond the broken window of Corina's house.

"We can't let him up here. He's too big and too strong for us to fight off," Corina continued. "I love him, but I don't want to die."

Sliding his arm around Corina's shoulders, Josh nodded his head. She leaned against him for comfort and he wondered if he could be as strong as she was. If Corina was bitten and he knew it, would he leave her to die alone or invite her into his safe haven and risk all of them?

Looking over at his brother, he felt his heart beat a little faster. The moonlight glinted off Drake's curls and Josh felt a pang of love for his brother so deep it surprised him. The little turd drove him crazy, but he really did love him. For all he knew Drake was the only family he had left anymore. Corina was right. He had to protect him.

"I just wish I could say goodbye to Brad," Corina said softly.

Josh didn't know what to say, so he stayed quiet. Her hair was very soft against his neck. It was a little distracting, but he felt like a grownup as he comforted her.

They sat in silence, watching the empty window Brad had disappeared into as well as the street. Slowly, the zombies began to return, wandering beneath the street light and through the bushes surrounding the houses. They walked more slowly and stiffly than before. Their coordination was significantly different from earlier in the day. A few even tripped and fell as they tried to step over the curbs and onto the lawns.

Josh felt relieved that the zombies were slowing down. It was a good sign. Maybe rigor mortis was setting in or something. They were a lot slower and clumsier now.

"He's not coming out."

Josh stirred, realizing he had been close to falling asleep. "Has it been a long time?"

Corina looked down at her cellphone and checked the time. "Thirty minutes."

Josh rubbed his chin thoughtfully before he got an idea. Grabbing a bobble head toy off the floor, he let go of Corina and stood up. Using his best pitch, he threw the toy as hard as he could at the open window across the fence. It sailed through the night and right into the darkened house next door. He could barely hear it hit the floor or wall inside Corina's home.

"What are you doing?"

"Seeing if he's in there hiding and at least warning him of the zombies." Josh shrugged not telling her the real reason. He was hoping he was wrong.

To his dismay, he was not.

Brad appeared at the window looking disoriented. He was moaning softly, his glazed expression telling the truth of his fate. Brad had died inside the house and resurrected.

Corina lowered her head and began to weep softly. Josh sat back down beside her and took her hand. She rested her head against his shoulder.

Below, the zombies wandered through the night as Brad stood framed in the window, moaning softly.

Josh reached over to lower the shade, quenching the pale light of the moon that had filled the tree house. They had both seen enough death for the night.

"I think my mom and dad are dead. Probably my stepmom and stepbrother, too." Corina sniffled.

"I'm sorry," Josh answered in a low voice.

"I'm sorry about your mom."

"Me, too."

"Maybe we're all orphans except for Yessica," Corina sighed.

"My dad will come," Josh assured her. "My dad will come."

"I hope so. I really do."

They stayed sitting side by side in silence, holding hands, until it was time to rouse Troy.

Josh lay down on a blanket near the doorway after handing Troy the flashlight. Troy took up the post near the window as Corina lay back down with Drake.

As sleep dragged him down, Josh reached out and touched Corina's fingertips with his own.

CHAPTER 20

Josh woke with a start. "Mom?" He had dreamed she was calling him, telling him to get up for school.

Sunlight tried to push its way around the window shade. The cover over the door was torn free and hanging from one corner. Josh rolled over and looked down through the doorway.

His zombified mother growled and lashed out at him with one clawed hand. Gasping, he scrambled back before he realized she couldn't reach him. They were up too far. She was at least ten feet below. Edging toward the door, suddenly terrified that she was climbing up the ladder, Josh dared to look down again.

The zombie banged her hands against the trunk of the tree, growling. Her nails were torn and ragged from clawing at the trunk. The gun was no longer in her hand.

Wondering how she had gotten out of the house, Josh looked toward the back door and was surprised to see it ajar. His gaze swept over the yard and to the back gate.

It was open.

Standing up, he backed away from the door and looked around. Troy was asleep near the window, his head resting against the wall. Sam was snoring loudly, his mouth open. Yessica was curled up next to him, hogging most of the blanket that had covered them. Corina was spooning Drake, her arms protectively around him as she slept. There was no sign of Roger.

Looking down again, Josh saw that Arturo's

body was pulled toward the playscape. It was still covered. His zombified mother had no interest in the body. He had a feeling Roger may have dragged it there. Maybe Roger had been trying to drag it toward the alley. It made no sense. The wheelbarrow was pulled away from the door with the rocks still inside.

"Corina," Josh said softly. "Corina, wake up."

Slowly stirring, she forced her eyes open. "Mom?"

"No, it's me, Josh. Roger is gone. My mom is out of the house, and the back gate is open."

She sat up sharply, awareness filling her eyes. "Crap!"

"Troy, wake up! Rog is gone," Josh said, nudging Troy's leg with his foot.

Waking up with a start, Troy stared at him in confusion. "Huh?"

"Rog is gone. The back gate is open and my mom is out of the house. I think he might have let her out."

Josh couldn't wrap his mind around these events.

It was bad enough seeing Arturo and Brad turn into zombies last night, but this was really bad. Keeping the backyard clear had been an important part of them hoping for rescue.

"Is my daddy here to get us?" Yessica asked as she pulled herself out of her deep sleep.

"No, Yessica. It's something else," Corina answered.

Sam crawled over to the doorway and peeked out. He drew back, a horrified expression on his face. "Dude, your mom! She used to be so hot!"

Corina and Josh both hit him at the same time.

"Oww!" Sam frowned, grabbed a bag of chips out of the hollow of the tree, and retired to his corner to eat.

Drake sat in silence, staring at nothing. He looked disoriented and Josh moved to keep him from looking out the doorway. With a loud sigh, Drake crawled onto Corina's lap, laying his head on her shoulder.

Troy stared out of the doorway at the growling zombie. In silence, he drew the heavy plastic back over the doorway and tried to rehook it over the nail that had held it in place. It took a little effort, but he got it to stay back up.

"Maybe if she can't see us, she'll go away." Troy sighed and grabbed up a small box of animal crackers to eat.

Yessica crawled over to sit next to Corina. She pulled out her inhaler and took another hit. Josh wondered if it was good for her to be using so much of it. He could hear the little girl wheezing.

"Are we going to go find Rog?" Sam asked after a short stretch of silence.

"No point," Troy said sullenly. "He didn't want to be here anyway. He kept talking about going home last night. I guess that is what he did."

"He's probably a zombie," Sam decided.

Troy gave him a sharp look, but said nothing.

Corina motioned to Josh to get her a bottle of water and he moved to comply. He passed out water to the remaining survivors, startled at their diminished numbers. With Arturo and Roger gone, the group seemed so much smaller.

Despite the growls of his zombified mother below, the kids ate their breakfast of snack food and warm water. Corina struggled to get Drake to eat something, but the little boy kept his lips pressed together and refused to even take a nibble. Even Josh's begging did no good.

"What are we going to do?" Corina asked in a soft voice, eating the legs off an animal cracker.

Listening to the zombie growl below, Josh shrugged. "I'm not sure yet."

"C'mon. You're the freaking living dead boy," Troy said sharply. "You're the fearless leader of the Zombie Hunters. You gotta have a plan."

Swallowing hard, Josh frowned at Troy, but then realized Troy was serious. Looking around at the faces turned toward him, it became very clear to him that they were all looking to him to save them and keep them safe. He wasn't sure why. He had failed Arturo and Roger.

"You always have a plan," Corina finally said. "You always figure it out. Like last night with Brad. You knew he was a zombie when you threw the toy in the window, didn't you?"

Nodding, Josh ate a few more cookies, then looked toward Troy. "I screwed up with Arturo and Rog. I didn't keep them safe."

"Arturo lied and Rog went crazy," Troy answered. "But you took care of Arturo and I fell asleep letting Rog sneak out. It's my fault he's probably..." Troy looked down, irritated by his own tears.

"You killed two zombies yesterday, dude," Sam pointed out. "You're the hero."

"I'm a kid."

"A kid who is a hero," Corina responded.

Drake looked at him, sniffling. "You're the bestest big brother ever. You saved me."

Yessica reached out and lightly touched his hand with her grimy one. "You saved me when everyone else ran away."

"You're the hero, dude," Sam insisted. "You're the leader."

"Yeah," Troy agreed.

"You are," Corina said firmly.

"Uh, huh," Yessica agreed.

"Like Superman," Drake added.

"So..." Troy looked at him straight in the eye. "What's the plan?"

Josh took a deep breath as his mind pondered the possibilities. He exhaled slowly feeling the pieces of the plan coming together. "Okay, this is what -"

The cellphone rang.

"Who has it?" Corina exclaimed.

Troy began rummaging through his pockets as Josh did the same. Corina felt her own clothes as the phone continued to ring. The growls from the zombie below grew more feverish.

"Hurry before they hang up!" Troy began shoving the bedding around.

"Hurry before more zombies come!" Josh yanked a pillow back from the wall and saw his phone. Snagging it, he saw the word "Dad" illuminated on the screen. His hand trembling, he almost didn't hit the right button to answer.

"Dad!"

"Josh!"

"Dad, oh, God! Dad, it's you!"

"Josh, Josh..." There were tears in his Dad's voice. "I've been trying to call you all night."

"I'm okay, Dad. I have Drake with me. We're in the tree house."

"Your mom?" There was fear in his Dad's voice.

Josh swallowed the hard lump in his throat, shaking his head. Realizing his dad couldn't see him, he answered, "One of them bit her yesterday."

Silence on the other end made him worry his dad had hung up, then his dad said, "Josh, we're on our way. We got a caravan of trucks, buses and cars out of Austin this morning. It was rough going, but we did it. We're going to head through the town. How clear is it? Can you tell?"

Standing up, Josh drew near the shade. Slowly, he drew it back. He gasped. "Uh, lots of zombies."

During the night, more zombies had arrived in the street. They were gathered around something on the ground, jostling each other to get closer. The street was filled with a small army of the undead. The kids were lucky they hadn't made it to the alleyway yet.

"In front of the house?"

"Yeah." Josh craned his neck.

He could see past Corina's house and the one beyond it to the side street. That road looked emptier. The zombies had obviously been drawn to the front of the houses by someone on foot. Josh thought of Yessica's dad coming to get them and felt his heart beat faster.

"Orange Street looks a little clearer. I think we can get to the street through the alley."

"Okay, here is what I want you to do. Stay in the tree house until I call again. It will be in about an hour. When I call, it will be just as we get to Orange Street near the house. I want you kids to run as fast as you can down the alley. We'll be waiting for you. Our bus is going to come for you. The rest of the caravan won't risk it, but my buddy Derrick is going to drive our bus into town. I need you boys to run fast."

"I got friends with me," Josh said quickly.

"All of you then. All of you run fast. Do you think

you guys can make it? The zombies are slower now. You can outrun them." His father's voice was firm, but full of fear.

"Yeah. We can do it." Josh thought of his zombified mom down below and tried to gulp down the hard lump in his throat. "We can do it."

"Wait for my call," his dad said. "Then run like hell."

"I will dad," Josh promised. "I'll get Drake to the bus."

Looking up, he saw all the kids staring at him hopefully.

"I'll get them all there," Josh vowed.

"I got to hang up and save my battery. I love you," Jamie Rondell said emotionally.

"I love you, Dad."

There was a click then his dad was gone.

"Josh? What is the plan?" Troy's expression was full of hope and fear.

"We're gonna get my mom back into the house, shut the gate, and wait for my Dad to call. And when he does, we're going to run down the alley to

Orange Street as fast as we can to his bus."

The kids stared at him with wide eyes and mouths open in surprise.

"We're getting out of here," Josh said firmly. "And I got a plan."

CHAPTER 21

Josh yanked on the pulley system his dad had rigged up between his bedroom and the tree house. It was taut and strong. He had never used it for anything heavier than his portable stereo, but he knew his dad tended to overkill when it came to building anything. The tree house was rock solid and safe, so it made sense that the pulley system was also. The thick rope was rough against his hand as he pulled on it again.

"You can't do this," Corina said from behind him.

Down below, his mother was in a frenzy, slamming her hands against the tree. Luckily, at some point she had dropped the gun so he didn't have to worry about it going off. He had considered dropping the food cans on her head, hoping to stun or kill her, but realized it wouldn't work. Instead, they had packed the food into a pillow case to take with them.

"Yeah, I can. I always do good with the rope climb at school." Josh wasn't about to be deterred by any naysayers. His plan was scary, but it would work. He knew it.

The backyard continued to be free of zombies, except for his mother. They were out of view of the swarm in the front of the house, but he was aware that once he was on the rope, he could draw more. It would take the zombies a while to get around the fence and to the gate, but he would have to be very, very fast.

"As soon as I get her to the back door, one of you has to run and get the gate shut. We need to keep the yard zombie free so we can escape when Dad calls." Josh ducked back behind the black plastic and looked at the other kids as they gathered around. "Keep out of sight. Don't make any noise. As long as they don't know we're here, we can keep the yard clear."

"I'll close the gate," Troy decided. "I'm fast. I can do it."

"Are you sure? I can do it," Corina offered.

"No, I can do it. My brother opened it. I should close it."

"As soon as she gets into the house and that gate is shut, close the back door, trapping her, okay?"

"Yeah, Josh. Got it."

"I'll close the back door," Corina said firmly. "That way Troy won't have to risk her turning back."

"Okay," Josh agreed, "but make it fast and get back up into the tree house. Once I'm done getting her to follow me into the house, I'll get her trapped in the kitchen, run back up the stairs, and come back across the line. Then we keep quiet until my dad calls."

"The zombies might see you on the line," Troy

said.

"I know, but I think the branches will keep me hidden."

Josh didn't want to tell them what his alternate plan was. It would upset them too much and he needed them focused. Rubbing his slick palms on his jeans, he took a deep breath. Kneeling down in front of Drake, he hugged the little guy. Drake wrapped his arms tightly around his neck and kissed his cheek.

"We'll be with dad soon, little dude."

"Okay," Drake answered. His little face was tear stained, but his eyes looked clearer. "Don't be a monster like Mama."

"I won't," Josh answered. "Obey Corina, okay?"

"Okay."

Josh stood up and briefly hugged Yessica. Sam gave him a hot, sweaty hug as well. Troy gave him a fist bump.

"Take care, dude," Troy said.

"You, too, Troy."

"Good luck," Corina whispered, then kissed his

cheek.

Josh surprised her and kissed her mouth lightly. He blushed deeply at his action, but he didn't want to die not knowing what it was like to kiss her. It was...nice.

Without another word, he pushed back the plastic door, grabbed onto the rope and scooted himself out of the tree house. He quickly swung his legs up on the rope and began crawling along the trembling line toward the house. It led straight to his room and he knew the window was open. He shouldn't have any trouble getting inside.

The rope creaked as he edged along it, hand over hand, foot over foot, dangling over the snarling zombie below. The tree branches swayed around him, leaves rustling softly with the morning breeze. The agitated moans of the zombies beyond his house threatened to fill him with fear, but he fought it back. Concentrating on the rope, he ignored the strain and pain in his joints and muscles as he slowly moved down the line.

The hissing and snarling of his zombified mother

below him sent chills flowing down his spine. If he fell, she would...

Josh fought back that thought. It was useless now. He couldn't be afraid. He had to save his friends and his brother.

The rope gave little shudders as he moved, his slick hands sliding slightly as he gripped it.

"Keep moving," he muttered to himself through clenched teeth.

Josh didn't dare to look down or look toward the house. He concentrated on the rope and only the rope. He had seen too many movies to know that freaking out right now would be really, really bad. If he saw the screws slowly coming out of the wood of the house, he would panic; if he saw the zombie below, he would panic; if he saw his friends watching him from the tree house, he would panic. He had to keep focused and do his job.

The job his dad had given him.

He was going to save his little brother and his friends.

Josh's head impacted hard with the side of the

house and he gasped, his grip on the line almost giving. His legs swung off the line and he slammed into the house. Below him, his zombified mother groaned and reached desperately up to him. Beside her was another zombie. It was Brad.

Arms burning, Josh pulled his legs up away from the snarling zombies and hooked them over the rope. This would be the hard part of his plan. Releasing the rope with one hand, he quickly rubbed his hand against his jeans to dry the sweat from it. Reaching out, he caught hold of the window sill. It was rough and dry against this palm. Once he was sure his grip was tight, he lashed out with his other hand as he let go of the rope with his legs. The momentum swung him hard against the house, nearly knocking the air out of him. He managed to get his other hand hooked securely on the window sill. He dangled there for a moment before scrabbling his feet against the clapboards of the house and pushing himself up.

Below, the two zombies groaned and beat against the house. It took a little more work than he had anticipated to yank out the window screen. His shoulders were screaming with pain and his legs quivered as he braced them against the house by his knees. The screen came off with a small screech and fell over his shoulder onto the zombies below. Daring to look down, he saw the zombies clawing at the house, unaffected by the screen slamming onto their heads.

Pushing up with his legs, Josh slid his body over the window sill and into his room. He landed on the floor at the end of his bed and took a deep breath. His hands ached and burned from the rope and his knees hurt, but he was inside. Forcing himself to stand, he looked out the window and toward the tree house. He could see that the plastic over the door was pulled back slightly and he suspected Troy or Corina was watching him. Otherwise, it looked like it was empty and abandoned; just how he wanted it.

Stretching his limbs, he was relieved to feel he could move without limping. Crossing his room, he picked up the heavy zombie killing bat he had gotten special permission from his dad to make. It had big nails pounded into the wood and looked like a makeshift mace. Holding it tightly in one hand, he opened the door and hurried into the hallway.

His heart beating hard in his chest, he looked down both short hallways in the upstairs part of the house. All the bedroom doors were closed and silence filled his home. Taking a deep breath, he started down the stairs.

When he had made his plan, he had not considered that maybe another zombie had gotten into the house when his mother had escaped. Holding tightly to the bat, he felt sweat began to pour down his back and bead on his forehead.

At the base of the stairs, the door to the study was open, the guns in the gun cabinet out of reach and no help to him. The entry hall to the side door was full of fishing and sporting equipment. The door to the downstairs bathroom was closed.

He darted across the hall and quickly pulled shut the door to the study. Breathing heavily, he forced himself to calm down.

The archway to the dining room beckoned to him, and as he stepped toward it, he cast a quick look down the entry hall to the front door. It was empty. Slowly, he stepped into the dining room and looked into the living room.

Empty.

He turned and moved toward the child gate still blocking the way to the kitchen. He sidestepped the overturned chair and took a deep breath. With shaking fingers, he reached out and pulled the child gate free.

The kitchen was dimly illuminated by the sunlight trying to press through the curtain at the single window over the sink. He lightly banged the bat against the edge of the doorway to see if anything stirred. The room remained still.

That left the laundry room.

That door was also open. Josh looked around the kitchen again, just to make sure a zombified Rog didn't jump out at him. He was pretty positive that Rog had come into the house through the outside door and opened the laundry door. That was what had let his mom outside. But of course, the back gate was open, so maybe Rog had run out after encountering the zombie version of Lynette.

Josh lifted his bat into an attack pose as he stepped into the laundry room. The small room was empty of anything other than the washer and dryer and the small table his mother had used to fold clothes on.

The back door was open, revealing the beauty of the sun-dappled back yard. It was a peaceful scene except for the two zombies wandering in from the back gate.

"Crap," he muttered.

That made four zombies he had to lure inside. Slowly, he stepped toward the outside doorway.

"Mom, Brad," he called out in a cracking voice.

His mother stepped sharply into view, startling him. He backed away from her, swinging his bat through thin air. She reached out with bloody, torn hands and pulled herself up into the house. Brad was right behind her. The two new zombies moaned loudly and staggered toward the house.

Josh backed further into the house, his bat at the ready. His original plan had been to trap his mother in the laundry room, but now there were four zombies to deal with and he realized he would have to lure them much deeper into the house.

His hands trembled with terror as he slowly stepped away from his shambling zombie mother. Zombie Brad pushed at her, trying to get past her, but Josh's dead mother shoved him back. The milky white eyes were devoid of all emotion, but her teeth clicked together with anticipation of Josh's flesh as she drew closer.

Over her shoulder, Josh saw the other zombies pushing their way up into the house as Troy and Corina climbed down from the tree house.

Moving backwards, he tried not to stumble. They moved through the kitchen, Josh a few feet in front of the staggering zombies. He pushed the stool his mom had used to get items up on the top shelves into her path. She didn't notice it until she tripped on it, falling into the stove. Zombie Brad stumbled over her, crashing to the floor as the two new zombies pulled themselves into the kitchen.

Josh reached out and snagged the doorknob to the kitchen door, ready to slam it shut. He had to be sure the back door was closed first or else the zombies would go right back into the yard and attack Troy and Corina.

Zombified Brad crawled on the floor toward him. Josh shoved the heavy cookbooks and flour tins off the counter onto his head. The zombie version of his mother was tangled up with the stool and trying to walk toward him. She fell again, kicking her feet. The two zombies behind her were people Josh had never seen before. They moaned with hunger at the sight of him.

The house abruptly echoed with the sound of the back door slamming shut. Relieved, Josh stepped back and shoved the kitchen door closed.

Brad's dead hand stopped it.

Josh shoved it again, but the zombie's body weight pushed on it. Josh's feet slid on the carpet as the door yawned back open. Zombie Brad's hand lashed out toward his foot and Josh leaped back.

He fell over the chair he had thrown the day before when he had been attempting to avoid his newly zombified mother's pursuit. Rolling over, he quickly tried to get his feet under him as the zombies spilled out of the kitchen toward him.

CHAPTER 22

The zombies snarled and groaned as they poured out of the kitchen. The ones that had once been Brad and Lynette were on their hands and knees, but the other two zombies were on their feet and much faster. Both were men, and they sidestepped the two zombies on the ground to lunge at Josh.

Josh got his feet under him and pushed off like a sprinter. He almost dropped his zombie killer weapon as he skittered through the archway, heading for the stairs. He felt the cold fingers of one of the zombies brush over his back as he ran and almost screamed in terror.

Hitting the stairs, he tripped again. Fear clawed at his insides, raked his brain, and stole all his breath from his lungs. The two new zombies were right behind him. The one in the lead grabbed his foot.

Flipping onto his back, Josh grabbed his bat and swung it hard into the creature's arm. He heard and saw the bone in the arm shatter. The zombie's grip loosened enough for Josh to pull free and crawl up the stairs. He could hardly breathe and his heart felt like it was about to explode. Reaching the top of the stairs, he looked back down to see the zombies struggling to get past the first few steps. They were on their bellies where they had fallen and clawing at the stairs. The other two zombies were back on their feet and heading toward the staircase.

Josh darted down the hall and flung open the door to Drake's room. He grabbed the rocking chair and dragged it back down the hall with him. Pushing it down the stairs, he watched it slam into the zombies below. In a frenzy of fear, he dragged other pieces of furniture back to the stairs and sent them tumbling down onto the zombies below, making it even harder for the zombies to make any progress. It took a few minutes and every chair and small table upstairs, but finally he was satisfied that they were pinned down and unable to move up the stairs.

Catching his breath, he realized he needed to do the one thing he was afraid of. He had to check and make sure that his friends would have a clear path to the bus when his dad arrived.

Moving into his grandparents' old bedroom, he ignored the musty smell and drew near the window. The curtains were drawn closed. He hooked his finger along the edge of the fabric, drew it back, and peered down.

What he had feared had happened. Zombies were on their way to the alley to get into the backyard. They had seen him on the rope and were coming for him.

The phone ringing beside him made him yelp and

he snatched it, breathing heavily.

"Josh!"

"Corina, I'm okay, but-"

"They're almost here. They're going to be here in ten minutes. They had to go another way to get to Orange Street because the zombies from the highway are in town. You need to get back here."

Josh looked down at the shambling creatures moving across the side yard of Corina's home. "I can't. The zombies are moving to the back of the houses. They saw me. I have to distract them. You guys go."

"Josh, no," Corina wailed.

"It's okay," Josh said firmly though fear churned in his stomach. "It's okay."

"No, it's not."

"I have to take care of you guys and my brother. I can do this." He hung up the phone and felt tears in his eyes.

Twelve seemed too young an age to die, but he had already watched Arturo die. Everyone seemed to think he was a hero. He knew that sometimes in the movies the hero had to die to save the rest of the people.

He shoved the window open and knocked out the screen. The zombies looked up at the commotion. They moaned when they saw him.

"Hey, stupid zombies! I'm up here! Not back there! Hey, stupid zombies!!"

The zombies nearing the alley turned slowly toward his voice.

"Hey, stupid dead guys! Looky! Up here! I'm up here!" He skirted around the bed and opened the other window, the one nearer to the front of the house. "Hey, look. Here I am!"

The zombies all moaned hungrily, reaching up toward him. Their dead eyes and terrible faces made him want to throw up, but he was too pumped full of adrenaline to stop now.

Running across the hallway, he opened up the window in Drake's room and busted out the screen. "Hey, dead guys! I'm up here!"

The zombies moving down the other side yard turned toward him. Eerily, they all raised their hands toward him and moaned.

Running back and forth between the two rooms, Josh drew the zombies toward the front of the house. Finally, he opened the windows in his parents' bedroom and watched with relief as the shambling, smelly undead of his neighborhood moved away from the back of the house and his friends into the front yard.

Screaming until his throat felt raw, Josh kept the zombies' attention directly on him. His zombie killer bat in one hand, he kept thinking about his little brother and friends. He had to give them a chance to survive or else he would have failed.

The phone kept ringing behind him and he ignored it. Josh knew it was Corina trying to stop him. He had to keep the zombies paying attention to him at all costs.

It stopped ringing, then started again.

Josh was touched by her persistence. He glanced over at the family photo next to his parent's bed and Drake's dinosaur, Rex, still lying on the bed where he had left it before leaving for daycare the day before. He had to do what he had to do. He couldn't let Corina stop him.

Now he would never know if she would be his girlfriend someday.

Finally, he picked the phone. He wanted to say goodbye one more time.

"Don't hang up! We're leaving. You need to get out here," Corina's voice said urgently.

"Tell my dad I love him," Josh answered. "I'll hold them off while you guys go."

Josh slammed the phone down and ran down the hall to his grandparents' room. Looking out one of the windows, he could clearly see the alley and Orange Street. Keeping behind the curtains, he saw a big green metro bus from the city of Austin slowing down as it neared the alley. Below, his friends and little brother opened up the back gate and ran into the alley. It was clear, thanks to his hard work, and he watched them run toward safety.

Zombies began to move toward the bus, the sound of its engine drawing them. Dashing back to the front of the house, Josh leaned out of the window and began screaming. A chunk of the zombies moved toward the bus. Below him, he heard glass shatter as the zombies busted out the windows of the house. They were coming for him.

Running back to the other room, he looked out to see his father pulling Drake into his arms and into the bus. Troy climbed on next. Yessica suddenly ran toward one of the zombies. Josh could hear her calling out for her father even from this distance. To his amazement, Sam ran after her. Valiantly, Sam shoved a slow moving zombie away from the little girl, his weight adding enough force to knock it to the ground. Then he grabbed the little girl's hand and dragged her back to the bus.

Josh felt tears running down his face as relief filled him. His friends were almost away and safe.

Then, to his horror, Corina turned and ran back down the alley, avoiding the few zombies shambling toward her. He saw her raise her hand to her face just as the phone next to him went off.

He grabbed it.

"Corina, go back!"

"Get out of the house now! I'm getting Brad's bike!"

Josh froze for a second, then suddenly he understood her plan. He grabbed his bat and ran out the door. Seeing Rex, he grabbed up the stuffed toy. He had promised Drake he would get him.

The sounds of the zombies coming through the broken windows downstairs filled the house as furniture crashed to the floor and glass shattered. Their moans filled the house and the stench traveling up from below made his eyes water.

From the sounds on the stairs, the zombies were finally making progress in their pursuit of him. Josh ducked into his room and grabbed his emergency lighter off his desk. Lighting it as fast as his trembling fingers would let him, he set his pillow on fire. He waited for a few seconds then threw it at the door.

Climbing out the window, he heard the sounds of the motorcycle roaring toward the house. Looking over, he saw the bus was gone and Corina was speeding down the alley toward his house. He tossed Rex and his zombie killer bat to the ground below.

Scooting out the window, Josh grabbed hold of the window sill and let himself down until he was dangling from it. Taking a deep breath, he dropped down to the ground, remembering to tuck and roll so he wouldn't break his legs. He still landed hard and his hip hurt, but he got to his feet. Grabbing up Rex and his zombie killer bat, he headed toward the gate that was standing ajar.

It burst open as Corina roared in. He was surprised to see she had a gun in one hand then recognized it as the one his mother had the day before. Corina must have found it in the yard.

He rushed over and climbed onto the back of the motorcycle. Holding onto his bat, he tucked Rex between their bodies and slid his other arm around Corina's waist.

"You got Rex!"

"I can't let Drake down," Josh answered.

Lifting the gun, Corina fired a shot at a zombie trying to follow her into the yard. It fell back out of view.

"Hold on!"

Corina gunned the engine. The motorcycle shot out of the yard and into the alley. All around them zombies reached out to grab them. Only their speed and Corina's expert handling of the bike kept them from being snagged from the wildly grasping hands. Josh slammed his bat into the face of a zombie trying to lunge for him as the motorcycle roared onto Orange Street and turned away from the zombie crowd moving toward them from the intersection.

Zombies shambled through yards and around the wreckage of cars as the two kids rode through town on Brad's motorcycle. Corina was fearless with her handling of the bike, and she kept them away from the thicker packs of the zombies. The dead were everywhere.

Up ahead was the big green bus that his dad and brother were on. Corina followed it as it roared out of town. The bus slammed through clusters of zombies and flattened any in its path. The motorcycle sped along behind it, weaving through the bodies

A few times Josh thought for sure one of the zombies would snatch them off the bike, but they escaped every time. A few times he used his zombie killer bat to shove zombies away. It was a journey through hell. He clung to Corina as she rode through it like a knight on the shiny motorcycle.

At one point Josh saw a familiar shape and turned to see Roger staggering toward the bike. Behind him, was Roger and Troy's zombified mother. Roger had found his mother after all, Josh thought sadly. Corina sped the bike up and they roared past the zombie Roger.

The buildings and houses of the town gave way to tall trees and the zombies were no more. They had escaped.

A long, winding country road unspooled before them. Looking over his shoulder, Josh saw smoke rising over the town.

The bus slowed down as it came to a stop. Corina rode up beside it just as the doors opened. Jamie jumped out of the bus and rushed toward them.

"Josh!"

"Dad!"

Jamie yanked Josh into his arms and held him tight. He kissed his son's cheek firmly and buried his face in his neck, sobbing.

"Dad, I'm okay. I promise. I'm good." Josh felt as though his heart would burst with happiness, but he was a little embarrassed at the same time.

Jamie cupped Josh's face in his hands and grinned. "Yeah. You are. You're so brave. You did such a great job."

Big massive trucks began to rumble up the road along with buses and some cars. It was the caravan.

"I did my best, Dad."

"And you saved them." Jamie turned to Corina. "And you saved Josh. Thank you."

Corina grinned before she was drowned in Jamie's embrace. Jamie watched as the big vehicles full of people slowed down.

"Come on. We need to get moving," a black man said from the doorway of the bus.

“We’re coming, Derrick,” Jamie answered.

A Labrador peeked her head out the doorway and woofed at them.

“Get back inside, Bonnie,” Derrick ordered, smiling.

A big man with a cowboy hat and another man dressed in a business suit walked over and took hold of the bike.

“I’ll load this up on the back of my truck,” the big man said.

“Thanks,” Corina said, picking up Rex from the ground. He had fallen when Jamie had grabbed Josh.

Jamie took hold of both of the kids by the backs of their necks and guided them toward the front of the bus. “We’re going to keep going out into the countryside and find a safe place. Army guys are on their way to join us. Coming up from San Antonio. We’ve been talking to them on the CB.”

“Dad, about mom...”

“We’ll talk about it later,” Jamie answered, pain in his voice. “I’m just glad my boys are okay.”

Josh stepped up into the big rumbling bus and looked over at the other passengers. A pretty young woman with long brown hair seated near the front with Bonnie pressed into her side. The woman was obviously blind. The dog watched them with curiosity. There were young and old people on the bus. All looked scared, but also relieved to be moving on.

Sam sat with Yessica in the seat behind the bus driver. His beefy arm was slung over her shoulders as he comforted her. He had saved her from her zombified father and looked a little older and calmer than before.

"Josh, you made it. Cool!"

"I saw you save Yessica. Good job, Sam. You're definitely a Zombie Hunter," Josh replied.

"Thanks, Josh. Are we friends now?" Sam asked hopefully.

"Yeah, dude. We're best friends," Josh answered.

Sam's smile nearly cracked his face in half it was so wide.

Troy sat near the blind woman petting Bonnie's

head. He gave Josh the thumbs up.

"Good to see you, Josh. You did good."

"Thanks, dude. I just wanted you guys to get away."

"It would have sucked if you died. Glad Brad taught Corina to ride his bike."

"I saw Rog," Josh started.

"I saw him, too," Troy answered, his sadness filling his eyes. "And my mom."

"We're your family now," Jamie told Troy firmly, leaning over to hug the boy.

"Thanks. I need one. Stupid Rog. Stupid zombies." Troy clung to Jamie for a few seconds, then drew away.

Corina handed Josh Rex and he moved over to where Drake sat sucking on his hand.

"Hey, lil buddy. Look who I found."

"Rex!" Drake's face lit up with delight as he snagged the battered stuffed toy from his brother. "He'll eat the zombies."

Corina looked at Josh sharply, a warning in her gaze.

"Yeah, absolutely. Rex will eat all the zombies," Josh agreed. He leaned over and hugged his brother, then kissed his cheek. "He's a good dinosaur."

Jamie laid a strong hand on Josh's shoulder, giving it an approving squeeze. "Absolutely. Rex helped Corina and Josh get here safely." He sat next to Drake, who immediately climbed onto his father's lap.

"He's the bestest dinosaur," Drake said proudly.

Corina and Josh exchanged small smiles as they slid into another empty seat. Drake smiled at Josh as he snuggled into his Dad's arms, Rex secure in his embrace.

"I love you, Josh."

"I love you, too, lil' bro."

The big front doors of the bus whooshed shut as Derrick took his place behind the driver's seat. The caravan began to move on and the big bus rumbled loudly as Derrick shifted gears.

"What's that?" Troy asked, staring back at the town and the black smoke rising above it.

"I set the house on fire to kill the zombies," Josh confessed.

"You did?" Jamie looked at him sharply.

"Yeah. They got in the house when I was trying to distract them so the others could get away. Sorry I burned the house down, Dad."

"Under the circumstances, I don't think I'll ground you." Jamie hesitated before saying, "What about your mom?"

"She was inside." Josh swallowed hard.

Jamie nodded, tears glistening in his eyes, but not falling yet. "Good job, son. May she be at peace."

Sinking back into his seat, Josh stared out at the trees and foliage speeding past the bus as it drove deeper into the countryside. Gently, Corina slid her fingers under his and he tightened his hand around hers. Turning his head, he smiled at her and she smiled back.

"You did really good, Josh," she said softly.

"So did you," Josh answered. "You saved me."

"And you saved us," Corina reminded him.

“We’re all heroes,” Josh decided.

“And survivors,” Corina added. She sighed softly, looking around at their friends once more. “Now we’re family.”

“Yeah,” Josh agreed. “A new family.”

His old life seemed far away now. He knew he would never see his old house or the tree house again. The school would stay empty and he would never attend class there again. He would never play with his best friend, Arturo, or Roger in his backyard pretending to fight imaginary zombies. He would never feel his mother hug him again or kiss his cheek.

It was all gone now.

Looking around the bus at all the other survivors, his friends and the remnants of his own family, Josh felt hope fill him. Maybe, he thought, maybe there was a chance for them all to survive now. And maybe there would be a good ending to his own personal movie called his life.

After all, he was now a real zombie hunter.

ABOUT THE AUTHOR

Rhiannon Frater works and lives in Austin, Texas. She became an Independent Author at the urging of her husband. She loves reading, movies, gaming, and hanging out with friends and family when she's not tapping away at her computer on her latest story. She also loves hearing from her fans and tries to respond to everyone who emails her.

She is the author of the **As The World Dies Zombie Trilogy** that was originally self published but was later picked up by Tor to be published in 2011.

She is also the author of the modern day vampire novel, **Pretty When She Dies** and the gothic horror novel, **The Tale on the Vampire Bride.**

To contact the author directly, email her at:
rhiannonfrater@gmail.com.

For more information on her writing, find her at:
www.rhiannonfrater.blogspot.com

8371744R0

Made in the USA
Lexington, KY
28 January 2011